# *Hard* LIMIT

the alpha antihero series

# SYBIL BARTEL

*Books by*
# SYBIL BARTEL

The Alpha Antihero Series
HARD LIMIT
HARD JUSTICE
HARD SIN
HARD TRUTH

The Alpha Bodyguard Series
SCANDALOUS
MERCILESS
RECKLESS
RUTHLESS
FEARLESS
CALLOUS
RELENTLESS
SHAMELESS

The Uncompromising Series
TALON
NEIL
ANDRÉ
BENNETT
CALLAN

# Hard LIMIT

the alpha antihero series

One fucking breath.

That's all I needed.

Air in my lungs so I could exhale through the pain.

My ribs broken, my face in the mud, one leg useless, I tried and failed to lift my head. Mosquitoes swarmed, and the sun dropped. I wasn't going to die out here. No fucking way. I was Tarquin Scott, and that was a hard limit.

But then I heard her voice, angel soft and breathless, and I wondered if I had been kidding myself. I didn't have time to figure it out. A small hand landed on my back, and I fisted my bloody knife.

I wasn't going to die tonight. But someone else was.

*HARD LIMIT is the first book in the Alpha Antihero Series.

The Alpha Antihero Series:
HARD LIMIT
HARD JUSTICE
HARD SIN
HARD TRUTH

# Dedication

For my Mom and my Dad,
even though I really hope they never read this.

"Candle was earth. Dark and dirty between your hands, he rubbed across your skin and left marks as his scent soaked into you like a memory. You smelled him after every rain, and you felt him every time you fell. He'd cradle you if you needed to lie down in the woods, but he'd never lift you up to touch the stars."

—Kendall, from ANDRÉ

# Chapter
## ONE

*Tarquin*

I SUCKED IN A LABORED BREATH AND SWAMP MUD FILLED MY mouth. Pain shot through my ribs as I choked. One cough and my head spun.

Spitting, panting short and shallow, I tried again.

A short inhale, and the stench of rot permeated everything. When I did not choke, I decided I did not care about the stench. My own body was rotting. Bloody, beaten, I used my good arm and leveraged my elbow. Digging it into the mud, raising my chest an inch, pain shot through my ribs and I heaved forward.

Army crawl. Or so I had been told.

One forsaken inch at a time.

I was going see another turn around the sun. I had to.

Dead people did not get revenge.

Dead people did not get anything except a hole in the ground.

That I knew.

I was a digger.

I had had one job on the compound. Bury the bodies.

Except I was not on the compound anymore.

Struggling for air, my lungs on fire, I heaved myself another inch. Mosquitoes swarmed, and I cursed. *"Fuck."*

The forbidden word rattled from my conscience and grew larger than the forsaken swamp. Then, just as I had been warned, the sin took hold, and more profanity bled out. "Fuck, fuck, FUCK!"

Stabbing pain stole my breath as my hoarse voice defiled the swamp's nighttime chorus, but I did not care. A laugh—half-gurgle, half-hysterical—ruptured from my chest like a rebirth.

"Born!" I yelled to the alligators, rats, and insects. *"Re-fucking-birth."* Coughing, rolling to my side, I blinked back mud until I saw the stars. The same stars I had seen every day on the compound, but I was not looking at them from there now. I never would. Not until I went back to kill every brother who had done this to me. Including him. "I'm coming for you, River Stephens."

Choking on my own blood, I coughed, and pain blindsided me.

I fell back to my stomach and forced the words out on a wheeze. "I'm fucking coming for you," I whispered to no one as my head landed in the mud. "You're—" I coughed. "—dead...." My chest burning, my leg throbbing, darkness edged out the night.

"Oh, *sweet Jesus.*" Like an angel, the female's voice floated down over me. "Are you breathin'?"

Was I dreaming?

"Can you hear me?" she asked, whisper soft and perfect.

No female had ever sounded that sweet. It was a trap, it had to be. Fighting an inhale, I willed my body to lie predator still.

"Oh Lord have mercy," she breathed, her voice heaven sent. "Please be alive."

A small, warm hand landed on my back.

Part animal, all instinct, my reaction was immediate. Palming my blood-stained, muddy knife, I reared up from the waist. I did not notice her hair was the color of summer sunlight. I did not notice her wide green eyes. I did not notice the freckles ghosting across her face and falling to her chest.

I wrapped my arm around her neck, pulled her against me, and brought us both back down to the rotten mud. The tip of my knife pressed against the vein on the side of her neck, and adrenaline-induced words snarled past my parched throat. *"Who sent you?"*

Tiny hands grasped at my muddied forearm in desperation as she struggled for lifesaving air. "No-no-no one."

My knife about to break skin, I squeezed her neck harder. "Who do you belong to?" No female wandered out here alone.

"My daddy owns this swamp."

No one owned this land. "Liar," I accused, putting more pressure on the knife.

"No!" she squeaked. *"Please.* I'm tellin' the truth."

I did not have time to respond. A water snake slithered over her bare legs and she screamed. Jerking in my grasp, her elbow made contact with my beaten ribs.

Excruciating pain lanced through my side and bile rose in my throat.

My knife dragged across her neck as I forced my broken body to twist so I did not choke on my own vomit.

My stomach heaved, then everything went black.

# Chapter
## TWO

*Shaila*

His death grip on my neck released, and I didn't pause one single southern second. Jumping to my feet, I stomped my boots in the swamp mud to make sure that snake was nowhere near me. Nothing like a slithering reptile to make you lose all fear of a half-dead man holding a knife at your throat.

My throat!

My fingers muddied, I dragged the back of my hand across my neck and held it up to the full moon.

No blood.

I glanced down at the blond man with muscled arms almost as big as my thighs. Stock-still and laid out like Jesus on the cross, he christened the muck all around him.

Holy hell.

He looked so pathetic, I couldn't even be mad at him for the knife. Wasn't the first time I'd seen a blade.

My gaze cut to his broad chest, but it didn't move.

I dropped to a squat and held my hand in front of his

nose. "Don't you quit breathin' on me." Please, *please* let him be alive.

Daddy would have my hide if I told him there was a dead man on his land that he didn't put there. If he didn't accuse me straight-off of being up to no good, he'd for sure ask why I was out here to begin with, and I couldn't let that happen. Not now, not when I was so close. I needed to keep my nose clean and make sure all my ducks were in a row. I was getting out of here soon, come hell or high water, and no funny-talking dead man was gonna stop me.

The man sputtered up a cough.

Relief exhaled through my own lungs, and I took his switchblade from his open palm. For a second I weighed having my prints on what could very well be evidence from whatever had happened to him, versus having him coming to and pulling the same stunt twice.

It wasn't even a choice.

I wiped the knife on his muddied pants as best I could and closed the blade before tucking it in my pocket. "Okay, mister, you need to wake up." I patted his cheek. "Come on, now. It's feeding time for the no-see-ums, and I'm fixin' to get inside."

He didn't move.

I upped the ante and slapped him.

Bright blue eyes popped open, and his hand went unerringly to my throat. "Who tends to you?" he barked.

*Holy shit, he has some kinda grip.* "Mister," I choked out. "If you don't let go, there's gonna be no one here to help you." I grabbed his wrist and dug my thumb and forefinger into the webbed skin of his hand.

He instantly let go. "No female should be out here alone."

"Glad you're chivalrous, but we can talk about that later. You need to get out of the mud and indoors before the no-see-ums suck whatever blood you have left." I stood up, but held my hand out. "C'mon, get up. Then you can crawl back under whatever rock you came from."

For one long moment, he studied me like I was the fish outta water. Then his scratchy voice, deep and rough like half-rotten wood, filled the night space between us. "I am not going back."

Huh. "Then you can go somewhere new." I wiggled my hand. I didn't have time for this. I needed to get back home.

He stared at my hand but didn't move. "Why would you help me?"

My hands went to my hips, wondering if I was biting off more than I could chew. If trouble arose, I knew how to shoot. But my shotgun was inside the house in the hall closet, and I didn't particularly want to trudge all the way back to get it, only to have to come right back out here to shoot his sorry butt. "You see anyone else willing to take on the job?"

"You should be afraid of me."

I laughed. "Mister, if I was afraid of every muscled man with an attitude, I'd have no business callin' myself Daddy's girl." Not that I did it often, but if the need arose, I wasn't beyond using it to my advantage.

The stranger's eyes narrowed. "Who is your father?"

"Who's yours?" I countered.

He hesitated only a second, but then a sneer formed on his full lips. "I do not have one."

I couldn't figure out if that made him lucky or cursed. Glancing at his shoulder that was bent at a funny angle, I decided on the latter. "Well, that's unfortunate, because right about now you're lookin' like you could use all the help you can get."

"Leave."

This time my laugh was more an unladylike snort than a chuckle. "And let you die on my land?" I shook my head and reached for his good arm. "I don't think so." My hands wrapped around his shockingly hard bicep and I tugged. "Come on, swamp boy. You're gettin' up." With no little effort, I pulled him into a sitting position.

He hadn't flinched when I pinched his hand, but this time, he let out a pained howl that rivaled a wolf on a full moon as he sat. Short breaths cut in and out of his lungs, and for a second, I wondered if I should've left him lying.

Still holding his arm, I squatted back down and risked putting my arm behind his shoulders. One of his legs was limp, his torso, where I could see past the mud, was all bruised and bloody, and his face was a roadmap for what looked like the wrong end of a fist, or three. Saying he'd been through the wringer was an understatement. "Maybe I should just call for an ambulance."

"No," he barked with surprising strength. "No doctors." He shrugged away from my arm.

"Fair enough." Who was I to judge? I'd never been to a real doctor in my life. "But you're gonna have to work with me then. In good conscience, I can't leave you out here, and I can't carry you back to the house, so you gotta move."

His gaze scanned the swamp. "How far?"

8

I nodded in the direction of the house. "Just past those trees on the other side of the clearing."

"Kilometers?" he asked, as if the amount of actual distance would make a difference.

"I don't know about nothin' fancy like kilometers, but if a yard's three feet, then I reckon we got a good few minutes' walk ahead of us. More if you're slow."

"I cannot walk," he stated without emotion.

I frowned. "Then how'd you get clear in the middle of the swamp? Someone dump you here?" Which, if it was one of the guys from Daddy's club, then I wasn't covering for him. I was telling Daddy, and he could deal with whoever thought they could leave their trash on his land.

The blond man's head turned, moonlight hit his face, and I got the full force of his unwavering stare. "I crawled."

Mud covering most of his face, one eye almost swollen shut, his lip split, I was still taken aback. Broken and dripping trouble, he was the most handsome man I'd ever laid eyes on.

Swallowing past the sudden dryness in my throat, my voice wavered. "You crawled? From where?"

Staring at me, he tipped his chin over his shoulder, indicating the land behind us.

I tried and failed to shake off disbelief. "There's nothin' out there for miles and miles, and past all that nothingness is a whole lot more nothingness of defunct orange groves that run along the perimeter of the Everglades. And if you ask me, those old groves only lose more footin' each year to the wild of the Glades. They should just give up already. Ain't nobody out there to pick 'em anyway."

His jaw ticked.

The slight movement in his otherwise stillness brought me up short. "You sayin' you came from there?"

He didn't nod, but he didn't shake his head.

"Well, I'll be." I sat back on my haunches and swatted at a mosquito as I dragged my eyes over his body. "You look pretty fit for a homeless person." I'd heard the rumors that homeless people lived off the land in the Glades, but I'd never met one.

"Leave," he said again, but this time quieter.

Despite the eighty-degree weather and humidity I wouldn't wish on my worst enemy, chill bumps ran up my back and curled around my neck. "Now see, I can't do that." I tested a smile on him. "Would you leave me here if you found me in your condition?"

Without hesitation, and with a dead seriousness that chilled me to my very bones, he laid four words on me.

"I would bury you."

# Chapter
## THREE

*Tarquin*

**M**OONLIGHT SHONE ON HER HAIR. IT WAS NOT BLONDE, BUT it was not red. Somewhere in between. I had never seen hair that color.

"Charming," she muttered, seemingly unfazed by my admission.

My energy waning, I tried one more time. "Leave. You do not belong out here." I did not know how many sunrises had passed since I had been thrown off the compound, or how far I had made it. I had been left for dead far outside the main gate, but if any of the hunters happened across me, I would have a bullet in my skull as fast as they could pull the trigger of their rifle. And with her looks, she would be dragged back to the compound.

The thought made anger spur.

Making a derisive sound no woman on the compound would ever get away with, she rolled her eyes at me. "If I don't belong on my own land, mister, then it's about as sad a day as it's ever gonna get, because I sure as hell don't fit right out there in the real world." She waved her hand dismissively behind her.

My pain momentarily forgotten, alarm spread. "Real world?" I felt for my knife, wondering if there was more than one compound in the area.

"Yeah." She half smiled, half frowned at me. "Life, boys, girls, normal kids goin' to college, bikers, clubs, parties—real world," she said plainly, as if it were obvious.

The only word I knew of in her rattled-off list was college. No textbook had ever touched my hands, and I intended to keep it that way, but I knew of what she spoke. "There is no compound on your land?"

Her head tilted and her hair caught the moonlight. "Come again?"

"Compound," I repeated, air wheezing in my lungs.

Her laugh was more ironic than humor. "You must've hit your head somethin' good. The closest thing to a compound out here is when Daddy hosts the summer barbeque and the whole club descends for a drunken weekend filled with more fightin' than prayin' at Sunday worship."

My jaw tightened at her last word.

Noticing, she nodded in commiseration. "I see that's about as appealin' to you as it is me." She tugged on my arm. "Come on, let's get you cleaned up and in better light. Then I can see what I can do about tendin' to your…" She waved her free hand again. "All of this."

No female was going to tend to me. I jerked my arm away. "I said *leave*."

"Fine." She slapped her hands on her thighs as if she were frustrated. "If your sorry, pathetic butt wants to rot here all on your own, be my guest." Pointing a finger at me, she positioned herself to stand. "But don't think for one second that I'm gonna let—"

I grabbed her hair and yanked.

She fell back with a yowl and landed in the mud.

Ignoring the pain that lanced through my body, I loomed over her as much as I could in a sitting position. "Watch your mouth, or next time you will not be walking away from me."

"Watch *my* mouth?" She kicked me in the shin. "You dirty, rotten, piece of—"

I pulled her hair hard.

"Ow!" Her hands went to my forearm as her leg shot out.

I barely avoided another kick. "Do it," I warned. "Kick me. See what will happen." I had enough fight in me. I could take a female.

Her fingernails sinking into my flesh, she did not hesitate. Her boot slammed into my knee.

Pain exploded and I grunted, but I did not let go of her hair. Shaking my head, breathing shallow, something came over me. "Is that the best you can do?"

One second she was pulling on my arm, the next, the fury of hell unleashed and she was everywhere.

Her leg swung over me, she straddled my waist, and her arms started flying. Her head bent, her hair caught in my punishing grip, she rained down blow after blow wherever she could reach.

My ribs, my chest, my thighs.

She hit. She kicked. She spit.

Desire surged.

Diabolical desire.

Swamp mud covering my face, the corner of my mouth twitched. "Hit me like you mean it." I thrust my hips.

Sucking in a sharp breath, I knew the exact moment she felt me between her legs.

"Do you like that?" I leered. "Do you need a man to tend to you?" I had never let any female ride me, and I was not going to start now. Vanquished, left for dead, and covered in rot, I still had my pride. "Is this how you think you are going to get it?"

"Let go!" She punched me in the ribs.

Air whooshed out of my lungs, and I grunted out a demand. "Take your clothes off." Beyond pain, desire made my erection throb. "Spread your legs." I would put my mud-caked mouth on her womanhood. "I will show you exactly how a man tends to a female."

"You sick son of a bitch!" Her palm jammed into my wounded shoulder.

A wail, hers, mine, shot through the night as my hand jerked, and I pulled her hair hard enough to snap her neck.

I fell back, she landed on top of me, and my grip released.

Fury etched across her face, she glared down at me.

Suffocating in pain, I locked my expression and stared back.

Her hand fisting, she pulled her arm back.

I saw what was coming. "Do it." I had not survived River Ranch only to be taken out by a female. "Hit me as hard as you can, woman."

"My name's not *woman!*" Her fist sailed through the thick air. "It's Shaila!"

The crack of flesh connecting with flesh sounded a split second before my head snapped back. Fresh blood filled my mouth, and I sputtered before everything went black.

# Chapter
## FOUR

*Shaila*

GRUNTING, USING ALL THE STRENGTH IN MY ARMS, I WEDGED my boots in the mud and shoved. His stupidly big body rolled up a few inches.

It was enough.

I toed the piece of cardboard under him and let go.

He flopped back to the ground, landing mostly on my handiwork.

"You dumb shit, motherfucker." Out of breath, I kicked him. "That's for making me swear. Real ladies don't cuss like a biker." I brushed my hands off on my ruined clothing. "First you wreck my favorite jean skirt, and now I gotta drag you clear across the swamp." I bent and grabbed two ends of the flattened box I was using as a makeshift gurney and pulled as hard as I could. He moved three whole inches. "*Damn.* You shoulda died. A shovel is easier than this shit."

He didn't reply.

He couldn't.

He was out cold, and from the looks of him, probably staying that way.

"Fine." I spit out the taste of swamp. "Don't say anythin'. I don't care," I lied, feeling marginally guilty for punching him out. But that punch had cost me one set of swollen knuckles, so as far as I was concerned, we were even.

Panting, gripping the cardboard, I pulled two more times. The third tug, I hit a patch of weed grass and he slid a whole foot.

I let out a little whoop of victory. "Now that's what I'm talkin' about."

"Shaila?"

"Shit," I whispered, freezing in my tracks before calling over my shoulder. "Yeah, Mama?" What the heck was she doing up?

"Where are you, sweetheart?"

Damn, damn, damn. "Just out past the yard." I flicked the flashlight in my pocket off. "Thought I heard a baby deer cryin' when I took the garbage out," I lied. It wasn't a deer. It was a man cursing up a storm, and I wasn't just taking the trash out. I was hiding supplies in the garage.

"Well, leave it be and come back in. It's too dark and too buggy out there. You'll get eaten alive."

Of all nights she chose to make a fuss over me. "Just a few more minutes, Mama. Go on in, I'll be there soon enough."

"Okay," she relented. She hated the woods around the property more than she hated living where we did. "But make it quick. Your daddy will be here soon."

"He's not coming this week." He said so last week when he'd made his routine Sunday stop to look in on me and Mama.

"He just called. He said he's coming tonight."

*Shit, shit, shit.* "Be there in a sec!" I hollered, tugging again on the cardboard. "Go in before you get bit up!"

No wind to speak of, sound carried across the swamp, and I heard the back door shut.

"Okay, mister, let's do this." I needed to get him out of the way before Daddy saw him.

Daddy said he kept me and Mama out here so we could live in peace and keep an eye on his land, but he was lying. Mama couldn't be trusted around the club, and Daddy was keeping me away from the bikers in his MC until I turned eighteen. He'd told Mama last year he was gonna trade me up.

I wasn't no book scholar, but I wasn't stupid neither.

I knew what that meant.

He was gonna auction me to whichever dirty biker'd pay the most for the club president's virgin daughter.

But I wasn't gonna let that happen.

A few more paychecks from the gas station down the street where I worked, and a few more stolen supplies, and I'd have enough to escape and hold me over for a year, maybe two, until I figured out what to do next. Not that I wanted to leave Mama, but what loyalty did I owe a woman who'd brought me up in an MC clubhouse while she was busy spreading her legs and getting high until she took it too far?

Now we were out in the middle of a swamp, and she lived her entire life for one hour a week when Daddy would come by, pretend to be her faithful lover, then disappear after she serviced him. She didn't care about him selling me off as long as he kept coming to give her the new kinda fix she'd traded for her old one.

I suspected that after I turned eighteen, Daddy wouldn't need Mama anymore. But just in case, I wasn't gonna rock the boat before I had to. So here I was, dragging a half-dead man to our garage because I didn't want to cause no trouble with Daddy.

But as I looked down at the blond-haired man with more muscle than sense to not get beat all to hell, I thought about his stark blue eyes and that feeling between my legs I ain't never felt before, and maybe, *just maybe*, I was lying a teensy bit to myself.

"Come on, mister," I grunted, yanking him another few yards. "I don't got all night."

He didn't respond, and I kept pulling.

What felt like hours later, I dragged him across the yard and into the old garage that was more barn than garage because we didn't have a car. Another thing Mama couldn't be trusted with.

Stopping to catch my breath, I turned on the light and gave the stranger a good once-over.

The first thing I noticed, besides the fact he was wearing only jeans and heavy-looking boots, was that his arms were even bigger under the single overhead light.

The second was that he was tall.

And for all his hair-pulling, smack-talking, tough-act routine, he looked peaceful as a baby sleeping.

A baby who'd ruined my best skirt.

"Hmph." I grabbed the hose. "This is gonna hurt you more than it'll hurt me. And trust me, I'm gonna enjoy that."

19

SYBIL BARTEL

I turned the water on and sprayed him down like a dog.

Five minutes later, after leaning over and rinsing the gunk out of my own hair, I stood there gaping.

He wasn't no dog.

He was a god.

A gorgeous, perfectly built, muscled display of bruised hotness. With... *dang*... two stab wounds. One on his leg right through his jeans, and one on his side, both of which I needed to get washed up and stitched because they were oozing, and that didn't look too good.

I'd seen worse. Way worse growing up around bikers. From gunshot wounds to road rash to beaten to a bloody pulp, I'd seen it all. But the fact that I was now staring at a larger-than-life, hot-blooded man and found all his wounds attractive was probably something I should've been worried about.

Except I was too busy staring at his snug-fitting jeans.

"Ohh, girl." I shook my head, talking to myself. "You do not have time for those kinda thoughts." I needed to clean up his cuts and fix his shoulder that was popped out like Mama's was that time she fell in the shower.

Sighing, I kneeled next to him and picked up his forearm. "Trust me," I murmured. "I watched the YouTube video a dozen times before I tried this before. We should be good." Feeling up his arm, holding behind his elbow, I exhaled.

Then I twisted as I pulled.

His shoulder popped back into place with a sickening little click, but he didn't even flinch. I felt bad for pushing on it earlier in self-defense, but his breath was moving in and out of his lungs evenly and he seemed to forgive me.

20

I sat back on my haunches. "Well dang, oh for two." Sweat slicked my brow. "You're welcome."

No manners, he didn't reply.

"Fine." I stood. "You can thank me later." Stomping my boots, I tried and failed to get the mud off. "Shoot. I can't very well clean you up and stay dirty myself. You're gonna half to wait here while I grab the first aid kit, a quick shower and some soap for those wounds."

I coiled the hose and, as an afterthought, took an old horse blanket and folded it before putting it under his head. "Stay put. I'll be back before you know it."

I turned the light off and pulled the warped door shut before heading back toward the house. I was a few paces from the front steps when Daddy's SUV came around the bend and sped down the drive.

Caught in the headlights, my heart slammed into my throat.

I didn't bother making a run for the house.

The tires spun as Daddy's driver braked too fast, and the passenger door opened.

"Shaila," Daddy tsked, but with a disarming smile. "Your hair's wet and you're covered in mud, girl." His shoulders squared, his hair perfectly trimmed, his jeans pressed, he didn't look a thing like a biker. He never had.

"Hi, Daddy." Careful not to touch no part of my dirty self to his clean clothes, I stood on tiptoe to kiss his cheek. "Mama's inside. I was just goin' to shower and clean up." I backed away, hoping like mad he didn't ask any questions.

"Ah, ah, ah." He grabbed my upper arm. "Start talking." His eyes narrowed. "It's after dark. You know how I feel about you being out after sundown."

21

*Shit on a cracker.*

I wasn't so naïve that I didn't know the difference between real concern and him keeping me pure, but I played the game anyway and forced a smile. Stone Hawkins was not a man you wanted to cross. "Just thought I heard a baby deer cryin'. You know I couldn't leave a little ole baby alone and in distress all night."

Daddy chuckled and pinched my cheek like I was still ten. "That's my girl." He looked over my shoulder toward the house. "Where's your mother?"

"Inside." I glanced toward the house. "Probably at the window watchin' and waitin' on you." The woman had no self-respect.

Pulling two bags of groceries out of the back of his SUV, Daddy chuckled. "She is consistent." He handed me one of the bags. "Take that inside and clean up. Make your mother dinner."

It was almost ten o'clock. I didn't tell him we'd already ate. Time meant nothing to him. "Yes, sir." I turned toward the house.

His hand landed on my shoulder and he squeezed hard. "Your birthday's coming up in a couple weeks."

His breath touched the back of my neck, and I fought a shiver. "Yes, sir."

He dropped his voice to a stern tenor. "You still a good girl?"

I swallowed back bile. "Mm-hmm."

"Good." He slapped my shoulder like I was one of his bikers. "That's good, girl, because I've got a surprise for you. Now, go get cleaned up. Give me and your mother some time alone."

# Chapter
## FIVE

*Tarquin*

CHOKING.

No breath.

Air hitched in my lungs and I coughed.

Sucking in through my nose, I rolled.

Stabbing pain shot from my ribs, and I vomited water.

*Water.*

Cold. Wet. It dripped down my face. My teeth started to chatter.

I forced my eyes open.

Pitch black.

Every forsaken breath hurt.

Fuck.

*Fuck.*

The female.

I listened for a moment, but heard nothing.

My pants soaked, my hair wet, I was lying in a puddle.

Shivering, not knowing if I was dead, I closed my eyes.

# Chapter
## SIX

*Shaila*

SITTING ON MY BED, FIDGETING, I LISTENED TO THE DISGUSTING sounds Daddy made with Mama in her room.

"Oh good Lord," I whispered, rolling my eyes. "How long are they gonna carry on like that?"

I got up and looked out the window toward the garage. Still no lights on, the door hadn't spontaneously popped open. Not that I thought the stranger was gonna wake up anytime soon, but still. I didn't want nothing to happen while Daddy was here. He'd make sure Mister Blond-Hair would disappear, but I was already plotting.

If he'd come from the Glades, and he'd lived back there, then maybe he'd be of some use. I wasn't keen on going out on my own, but I couldn't stay here. Living in the small abandoned shack I'd found last year deep in the woods wasn't the life I wanted, but it'd be my life. I wouldn't be at some biker's beck and call, and I wouldn't be dragged into club life.

And if I was careful, maybe I could still come and check on Mama every once in a while. She hadn't been a real mama to me since I was five years old and I took care of her for the first time while she was sick from alcohol poisoning, but she was the only family I had besides Daddy. And it didn't take a genius to figure out Daddy was about as loyal as a Vegas winning streak.

Not that I'd been to Vegas.

"Shaila!" Daddy hollered up the stairs.

I popped my head out my door. "Yeah, Daddy?"

"Get down here, girl."

"Comin'!" Nerves rattled, I slid the first aid kit under my bed and closed my bedroom door behind me before hurrying downstairs.

Zipping his pants, not even trying to hide what he and Mama had been up to, Daddy waited for me in the living room. "I talked to your mother."

Mama walked out of her bedroom in a robe and nothing else. With a faraway look on her face, she smiled.

I crossed my arms. "About?"

Daddy buckled his belt and focused on me. "You're a grown woman now. It's time you take responsibility and contribute to this family."

Anger stirred. "I already got a job. I bring in—"

Daddy held his hand up in warning. "I'm not talking about your job behind the register at the gas station. I'm talking about your responsibility to grow this family and make it stronger. I'm talking about what you owe me and the club." He smiled like he was about to offer up the keys to the kingdom. "It's time to introduce you to someone."

Dread washed over me, but I forced a smile. "This isn't the dark ages, Daddy. Girls don't need their daddies to set them up. Besides, I got plans to go to college," I lied. I didn't need a fancy degree, but if it'd get me out of this without having to run to the woods past the swamp, then all the better.

Daddy laughed. "You didn't even go to high school. What makes you think you're going to college?"

I smarted. "I finished high school on the computer you gave me." Didn't take me but three years.

Giving me a condescending smile, he pinched my cheek. "Good for you. You're going to meet my friend Rush in a couple weeks." His expression turned cold, and he leveled me with a warning look. "You're going to be nice to him. *Very* nice."

My stomach lurched, and I sucked in a sharp breath through my nose so I didn't hurl my instant mashed potato dinner all over him.

"Please, Daddy," I begged. "Don't set me up with one of your biker friends."

I didn't want that life. I'd never wanted it. I saw what it'd done to Mama, and despite the scars on her forearms, she'd gotten off easy.

"*Biker friends?*" Daddy narrowed his eyes at me. "What do you think has put a roof over your and your mother's heads for all these years?" He didn't wait for me to respond. "It's not you." He jerked his chin toward my mama in disdain. "It sure as hell isn't her." His nostrils flared. "I do. My club does. My money pays for all of this." He spread his arm wide like we lived in the lap of luxury. "You had a privileged up-bringing. Now you're going to pay it back. Look nice in two weeks." He flicked my wet hair and scoffed at my clothes.

"Not like a drowned hick." Pivoting, he walked to the door. "In the meantime, take care of your mother." He left.

Mama exhaled. "He's such a good man."

My hackles went up, and I turned on her. "Good man?" Was she crazy? "He's as good as selling me to the highest bidder. That's not a *good man*. That's sick, Mama." I was done holding back for her sake. "He's selling his daughter's virginity, and you know it. What's wrong with you?" With every word, my voice climbed higher and my anger burned hotter.

Mama waved her hand through the air. "Oh, sweetheart, it was going to happen sometime. You might as well have a man who keeps you safe."

"*Safe?*" Was she insane? "How many bodies do you think are buried out here?" I wasn't no hick. I knew exactly why he kept this land. "You think being in an MC is a *safe* life? You think those barbeques where Daddy brings all the bikers out here with all their drinkin' and druggin' is *safe*? Name one legal thing Daddy's into, Mama. Go ahead, I dare you." Daddy ain't never held a real job a single day in his life. She knew it and I knew it.

A smile floated across her face. "But he's so handsome."

"Oh *my God*." I stormed over to her and grabbed her wrists. Pushing her sleeves up, I fought rage. "What'd he give you?" I demanded, checking her arms for the telltale marks. "What in the hell are you on? Answer me!"

She pulled her arms back and shooed me away. "Calm down, dear. He just gave a little pill, like he always does."

"*What?* Since when?" It'd taken years, *years* of hell to get Mama off the junk she'd gotten addicted to. It's why Daddy put her out here in the middle of nowhere. She couldn't be around the club. She couldn't handle the temptation. "You're not supposed to take anything!" She knew that. That was the deal.

"Oh relax." She pushed past me, heading back to her bedroom. "No harm ever came from a little pill. And I only ever take one at a time. Now, if you're done scolding me, I'm going to bed." She slammed her door shut.

A second later, I heard her bedside drawer creak open, and the flick of a lighter sounded.

I stood there until the scent of pot wafted into the living room. Then I inhaled the sickly pungent smell to remind myself.

I was never going to wind up like her.

# Chapter
## SEVEN

*Tarquin*

**M**Y BODY JERKED.

Sucking in breath, I came awake, and my teeth instantly started chattering. Blondish hair dragged across my shoulder, and the smell of something sweet filled my head.

"Gee, nice of you to join us," a female voice grunted from behind me.

My body jerked back a foot.

Dull pain spread across my ribs and I blinked.

"Nothing to say, huh?" she asked.

I fell to my back as the female, all legs and arms and reddish-blonde hair, scrambled out from behind me.

My throat burning, my head landed on a pillow, and my gaze settled on the female from the swamp. I narrowed my eyes.

Pushing one of my limp arms to my side, she squatted next to me. "Well, that's not a very nice thank-you. Especially since I even practiced my sewin' and stitched you up."

I forced a word out. "Water."

She smirked. "I shoulda known you'd be all demanding." Reaching behind her, she grabbed a bottle of water and brought it to my lips. "Not that I probably wouldn't be askin' for water after being passed out for two days."

Ice-cold wet slid down my throat and I groaned.

She took the bottle away and set it back down. "Easy, now."

I went to grab for it, but my arm, sluggish and heavy, made a slow arc instead of a calculated swing. "*Water.*"

"No, not yet. Give that a little bit of time to settle." Catching my arm, she laid it back at my side. "You're just gonna make yourself sick." She looked me in the eye. "I read that on the internet. I read plenty. So don't worry, I know what I'm doin'." She tucked a blanket around my body.

Following the graceful movement of her hands, I noticed I wasn't lying on the ground anymore. A mattress, filled with air, lay under me. My feet stuck out from the blanket she was fitting around me, and they were in socks I did not recognize. "Where am I?"

"In my garage." She adjusted the pillow under my head. "You were in bad shape. I couldn't very well leave you out there in the swamp to fend for yourself." She scoffed. "Lord knows how *that* would've ended."

I was not grateful. I did not say thank you. "Where are my pants?" With no material covering my legs, I felt my thighs sticking to the plastic.

"What's left of them needed a bath." She lifted the edge of a bandage on my jaw, nodded to herself, then removed the bandage. "But if I'm being truthful and all that, you need a new pair of jeans." Her gaze moved to my ribs, where she fingered a stiff white tape going around my torso. "You got broken ribs, you know." Her green-eyed gaze cut back to me. "Pretty sure I could feel them broken. Maybe just cracked." She frowned. "Okay, maybe just really, *really* bruised. Like you got kicked... *a lot.*" Crossing her arms over her knees, she squatted next to me and lifted one eyebrow.

I stared at her.

"You don't got nothin' to say about that either?"

I remained silent, but I took note that my eye was no longer swollen shut and my lip seemed healed.

"Huh." Inhaling, she narrowed her eyes. "Well, how about the stab wounds on your thigh and side? What about those? You gonna tell me how you got cut up?"

"No."

She made a snorting sound. "Fine. See if I care." She reached behind her to a bag and pulled an envelope out. "I bought these off Rooney. He sells anything. Well, anything you can take, snort or swallow. You'd think he could get real medicine easily enough, but it turns out, antibiotics are harder to come by. Took two days to get these." She shrugged. "Who knew?" Pushing out two pills from the folded envelope with writing all over it, she read the label. "You gotta take two today and one every day thereafter for four days." She handed me the two pills.

Cold, shaking, the blanket wrapped around me, I did not move. "I am not taking that."

She rolled her eyes. "Then how you gonna get better?" She nodded toward my leg. "You're shakin' because you got an infection in one of the knife wounds. Antibiotics fix infection. Everyone knows that."

I did not know that. "I have never taken them," I admitted.

"Well, now's as good a time as any to start." She raised a perfect eyebrow. "Unless you wanna die?"

I took the pills, swallowed, and choked.

Shoving me up to a sitting position, swatting my back hard, she made a derisive sound. "Now that was just plain dumb." She shook her head. "Men." Holding the water to my mouth, she cupped the back of my neck. "Drink."

My eyes watering, my ribs hurting, I gulped the water.

Satisfied that I had done what she said, she sat back on her haunches again and smiled. "There, was that so hard?"

I swiped a hand that was no longer covered in swamp mud across my mouth and lay back down. "What do you know about men?"

Her cheeks reddened. "Plenty."

Remembering her on top of me, my teeth ground. "Like?"

She dropped her gaze. "They're all stubborn and pigheaded."

My nostrils flared. "Do you speak to all men like that?"

"You always get beat up like that?" she countered, nodding at my body.

Rolling over in my makeshift bed, I issued an order. "Leave."

"Make me."

I had only been awake a few minutes, but in the meager light from the one overhead bulb, I had noticed every inch of her. The way her hips curved out from her waist. How her thighs were fuller than those of any woman on the compound. How her hair was shinier. How she spoke. How she made eye contact. How she smiled without reservation.

I had noticed it all.

And despite my ribs, side, and leg, I thought about holding her down and entering her from behind until the sun rose.

Looking over my shoulder, I gave her one warning. "Watch your mouth."

Ignoring me, she rolled her eyes. "You got a car?"

"Would I be here if I did?" I turned away again.

"Okay, good point." I heard her rummage in her bag. "You need to eat a little somethin', or those antibiotics will go right through you. And you ain't got a bathroom out here in the garage." She pulled on my shoulder.

Forced to roll to my back or use what little strength I had to stay turned away from her, I chose to face her. But when my gaze landed on her, I said what I needed to say with one look.

Unfazed, she held a sandwich out to me. "It's Spam. It's fresh. I just made it an hour ago, you don't need to give me stink eye about it." She picked up another sandwich for herself.

What the hell was Spam?

"Come on." She wiggled the food in front of me. "It don't bite." She smiled. "At least, not anymore."

Sudden hunger roared through my stomach. I did not know when the last time I ate was, and food was food, so I took the sandwich. Leaning up on the arm that hurt least, I inhaled a bite. Gagging, I almost spit it out. "Salt," I choked.

"Well, yeah, that's the best part. Spam bein' salty is

about one of the last things you can rely on in life." She took a bite of her sandwich.

"*Water.*"

Sighing, she reached behind her and handed me the water. "Fine, but drink it slow."

I gulped the whole bottle.

"Sweet Jesus." She shook her head. "If you vomit, I ain't cleanin' it up."

Ignoring her, I took another bite of the horrible sandwich. Two bites later, I had finished it and my stomach was not churning as badly.

With a knowing look, she reached in her bag and handed me another sandwich.

I ate it.

Watching me, she finished her first sandwich and set a new bottle of water in front of me.

Opening it, I drank half. Then I lay back down, pulled the blanket up, and closed my eyes.

She was quiet for half a second. "That's it? You don't got nothin' to say to me?"

"No."

"Didn't your mama ever teach you manners?"

"No."

"What's your name?"

I considered lying, but every part of my body was sore, and I was too tired to fabricate a name. "Tarquin."

"Tarquin?" she asked with surprise. "What kinda name is that?"

The kind a sick, ruthless, violent cult leader assigned. "My kind of name."

"Huh." I heard her slowly chewing. "What's your last name?"

No one went by last names on the compound because we all had the same one—his last name. But it suddenly occurred to me that I would never have to go by that surname again. I could have any last name I wanted. I could have had any first name I had wanted as well, but I had already given her mine.

I made up a new last name. "Scott." I had overheard one of the compound elders mention once that it was his name before he came to River Ranch. He had never done me wrong.

"Tarquin Scott," she repeated, slow and drawn out. "Well, nice to meet you, Tarquin. I'm—"

"*Shaila*," a female yelled from outside the building we were in.

I went on alert and my muscles stiffened. "Who is that?"

"My mama." Her eyes darted toward the door. "Be quiet. I'll be back." She jumped up and ran toward the door. "Coming, Mama!"

# Chapter
## EIGHT

*Shaila*

I RAN TOWARD THE HOUSE.

Mama was waiting on the front porch. Decidedly sober, she eyed the garage. "What's going on in there? You've been acting strange for two days."

I shrugged like it was no big deal. "Daddy told me to clean it up. I'm just doin' what I'm told."

She glanced back at the garage again. "Why do you have to do it at night?"

"What else am I gonna do? We live in the middle of nowhere."

She frowned. "Homestead isn't nowhere."

"We're not even in Homestead proper, Mama. You know that." I refrained from telling her she was the reason we were on the edge of civilization.

Avoiding confrontation, she opened the front door. "Come inside."

I hadn't seen it before two days ago, but I was seeing it now. Daddy had been giving her something for months, and now she was either out, or trying to stay off whatever he was pushing on her. Her hands fidgeting, her eyes darting around, she wasn't herself. Then again, if I'd been a better daughter, I would've noticed her glazed eyes and lack of any kind of fidgeting for the past few months.

But I hadn't.

Ever since I'd heard Daddy tell her again how he was gonna trade me up a few months ago, I'd been taking extra shifts at the gas station, stealing supplies and stocking the shack. All that busy work didn't go hand in hand with babysitting my junkie mother.

And now I had an even bigger distraction.

"I left the light on in the garage." I stepped back off the porch. "I have a few more things to pick up, then I'll be in."

Mama eyed me, then the garage. Then she said the first real thing she'd said to me in months. "I know you don't want to go with the man your father has in mind for you."

Shocked she was talking out of turn about Daddy, I didn't say a thing.

Inhaling, she stood in the open front door and met my gaze. "But your father has been taking care of me since I was your age, and I don't have any complaints."

Faster than a bobcat going after a rabbit, anger flooded me from head to toe. "No complaints?" *Taking care of her?* "You call a couple bags of groceries a few times a month takin' care of you?" I was incredulous. "Daddy doesn't take care of you, Mama." He never did. Not when she got addicted to the needle. Not when she was boozing her way through the club members. Not when she was half dead, getting ridden by two bikers at once on the pool table at the old clubhouse while she OD'd.

"You watch your tone, Shaila Victoria Hawkins." Just as quick as me, anger flared in her eyes. "Your father is a *good* man."

I went red hot. "A *good man* who doesn't take you to a proper facility to dry out, but hauls you out to the middle of nowhere with your underage daughter? Then leaves you with no car and no money, and dumps you here so you can dry out while my ten-year-old self stood by helpless to do anything but watch you almost die from withdrawal?"

"You do not speak about your father that way," she chided, her voice rising. "He got me away from all that!"

"He put you there in the first place!" I yelled back. "And now you want to condemn me to the same damn shit-for-nothing life you have!" I spun and stormed back toward the garage.

"Shaila Victoria, shame on you! You come back here right now!"

"Oh go smoke some pot," I snapped, yanking the garage door open.

"*Shaila.*"

"Leave me alone!" I slammed the garage door shut after me and locked it from the inside. Stomping my foot, I growled. "She is some kinda piece of work."

From across the room, blue eyes in a haunted face stared at me.

"Go ahead," I dared. "Judge me too."

His voice, all gravelly and rusty, came out of his chest sounding deeper than he looked capable of. "I am in no position to judge."

I smirked. "If I didn't know better, I'd think you were being sweet to me."

"I am not sweet."

38

I rolled my eyes. "No kiddin'. You're probably as bad as *Rush.*" I couldn't even say the stupid biker name with dignity. And I especially couldn't say it after having a name like Tarquin roll around in my mouth and float across my lips.

"Who is Rush?"

"Some biker my daddy's gonna sell me to." Not literally, but I knew the score. Money may as well exchange hands. That was, if Rush ever got his hands on me, which I had no intention of letting happen.

Tarquin's brow furrowed. "Sell?"

"Yeah." I crossed my arms and kicked at a crack in the old concrete floor. "Well, not for real money. More like for favors or alliances or something like that. My daddy doesn't ever do anything for free. Including lettin' the opportunity of his daughter's virginity go to waste."

Tarquin went very still except for the swallow of his throat. "You are not a woman?"

I laughed. "Oh, I'm all woman."

His frown deepened. "But you have not been taken?"

"Taken? This isn't kidnappers-R-us. Nobody's takin' me." Unless you wanted to get technical about Daddy giving me away to some dirty biker, then yeah, I would be getting taken against my will, but I wasn't gonna let that happen.

"How many turns around the sun are you?"

Wait. *What?* "How many what?"

"Turns around the sun," he repeated angrily.

"Okay, wait." My hands went to my hips. "Where you from? Cuz no one 'round here talks like that. I ain't ignorant, I know you mean to ask me how old I am, but you asked the question in about the strangest way I ever did hear."

"There is nothing strange about it," he snapped. "The earth revolves around the sun."

I stared at him a moment. "How many turns have you taken?"

He didn't hesitate. "Fifteen."

I burst out laughing and nodded at his well-over six-foot frame. "Mister, if you're fifteen years old, then I'm the Queen of England."

"You are not a queen."

Exactly. "And you're no fifteen-year-old."

He turned his head away, and for a long moment, I didn't think he was going to say anything more. Lying there still like a statue, his muscular arms at his sides, his long legs with his well-developed thigh muscles, he was all man. There was nothing teenager about him.

"I do not know how old I am," he quietly admitted.

"How is that even possible?" Where the hell was he from? "Did you grow up in the Glades?"

"Yes."

"And you don't know your exact age?"

"No."

"Your mama or your daddy never told you?" Was he off his rocker? "You got amnesia?"

"I do not know who my parents are. What is amnesia?"

Dang. "Amnesia is where you don't remember nothin' from your past."

"I remember everything."

"Except who your parents are?"

He sighed like he was put out. "You have one mother, one father?"

"Um, yeah." Ain't we all?

"I had many."

What the ever-loving heck? "What's that, like that TV show where that guy has a bunch of wives? What's it called, polygamy?" Was he for real?

He looked toward the door. "Was that your mother who called you?"

"Yeah. How many mamas you got?" Now I was intrigued. More than I should be. I'd never met anyone like him.

He ignored my question. "She will not come looking for you here?"

"She's afraid to leave the house."

He frowned. "Ever?"

I nodded. "Never." Moving closer to him, I sat beside the blow-up mattress I'd stolen from the gas station convenience store where I worked. "So tell me why you have a lot of mamas."

"That is how I grew up." His gaze drifted over my jeans. "Do you always dress like that?"

I laughed, I couldn't help it. "You're beat all to hell, cut up, infected and lying in a garage on a stolen air mattress, and you don't know who your mama is, but you're worried about what I wear?" The second the words left my mouth, instinct kicked in and it clicked. "Your family do this to you?"

His chest rose with an inhale, and despite him lying flat as a pancake, his shoulders went straight and proud. "I survived being vanquished."

"Vanquished." Now it was my turn to not know what the hell he meant. "What does that mean?"

He looked me in the eye. "I was cast out from River Ranch."

# Chapter
## NINE

*Tarquin*

ER EYES WENT WIDE, HER MOUTH OPENED, AND FOR THE first time, I heard her whisper. "Hot *damn.*" She stared at me as if I were an apparition.

I did not ask if she knew what River Ranch was. I did not have to.

"That's…. You…. *Shit.*" She shook her head and swallowed. "That's the most violent cult in like all of America. All of *history.*" Her hand covered her throat, and her voice pitched higher. "I hear they cut people up in itty-bitty bites and eat them."

"We are not cannibals."

She moved back from me. "But you cut people up?"

"I do not cut people up." I buried them after they were already dead.

"Well, that's a relief," she said sarcastically, before her mouth popped open again. "Oh my God! That's the branding on your back! The double R's, with one backwards, that's what that means, doesn't it?" She shook her head. "I can't believe I didn't even realize it. I mean, I saw it, but I thought, you know, your name was like Ron Roberts or something. But *River Ranch*? Oh, sweet Jesus, Lord have mercy." She scanned my body. "They did this to you?"

I nodded once.

"*Why?*"

"I gave a female a flower." I did not know why I told her the truth, except I was tired and sore.

"You gave. *A female*. A flower?" she repeated in stilted speech.

"Yes." I closed my eyes.

"Oh no." Her foot pressed against my leg. "You don't get to go to sleep after droppin' that kind of bomb. You need to tell me why they did this to you, and if they're gonna come lookin' to finish the job."

I opened my eyes and glared at her foot then her. "They will think I am dead."

She ignored the hostility in my stare. "The same way you think I believe you're only fifteen years old?"

The memory of River Stephens, River Ranch's founder and leader, standing over my prone body, telling the elders to beat me until I took my last breath, then toss me in the swamp replayed in my mind. I ground my teeth. "I am dead to them." I had held my breath and lain prone, not letting one sound escape during the last beating they gave me.

"Lord have mercy," she repeated low and quiet.

"There is no God." Not the kind I had been forced to believe in growing up.

She shook her head as if she felt sorry for me. "I wouldn't believe in Jesus either if I looked like you."

I changed the subject, not sure if I was more angered by her presence or intrigued. "I need to sleep."

"Oh, sure." She leaned over and tucked the blanket around me again then sat back. "Go ahead."

"What are you going to do?" I had never taken my sleep in the presence of a female.

Sighing, she looked toward the door. "Probably stay a spell." She looked back at me wistfully. "Make sure you don't stop breathin' in your sleep."

Did I need to worry about her suffocating me? "Where is my knife?"

She reached under the mattress. "Right here." Pulling her arm out, she held it up to show me, then she shoved it back where she had taken it from. "And for the record, it's rude to pull a switchblade on a girl."

"*For the record*," I repeated her saying, the words sounding ignorant and foreign, "do what I tell you next time."

She half laughed, half snorted. "You think I'm gonna listen to you?" She patted my shoulder and gave me a condescending smile. "How cute."

Vulnerable, undressed, unarmed, and wounded, I wiped my expression clean and lowered my voice. "Come here."

Without hesitation, she leaned toward me. "What's wrong?"

The scent of female and flowers settled around me and adrenaline surged.

I moved.

Grabbing a handful of her hair with my injured arm, I reached for her wrist with my other. Using my good leg, I leveraged my foot and brought her down at the same time I rolled. Hitting the cold cement floor, grunting through the pain in my ribs, I held her hair and her wrist and landed half on top of her.

She let out a gasp of surprise.

Using my weight to hold down one of her legs, I gave her a warning. "You kick me, I will make you bleed."

"With what?" Eyes wide, she didn't resist my hold, but her free hand grasped my wrist as I held her hair. "Your knife's under the mattress."

Dizzy, weak, my head spun with my sudden movement, but my body still responded to the female underneath it. Hard, I shifted my weight. "There is more than one way to make a female bleed."

Pink flushed her pale cheeks. "I'm not just a female."

"You are right." She was an untended female. One I was in no position to care for.

Her eyes narrowed. "What does that mean?"

"What do you think it means?" I used my waning energy to shove her thigh wide with my knee, and the full length of my desire landed between her legs.

She sucked in a sharp breath. "You need to get back on your mattress."

I pulled her hair, pressed down on her wrist, and thought about every way I wanted to enter this infuriating female. "Remember who you are speaking to, *female.*"

"I'm *speakin'* to a no-good, ungrateful jerk who needs to remember the *woman* he's threatenin' dragged his sorry ass half a mile across a swamp and SAVED HIM!" Raising her head despite my hold, she yelled the last two words at me.

It was instinctual.

My mouth landed on hers.

Punishing and hard, I thrust my tongue in.

I had never kissed a female.

Not on the mouth.

Angry, at her, at the world, I lashed through her intoxicating heat without reason or skill. Teeth gnashing, lips twisting, I stroked, I swirled, I demanded. I ate at her mouth like I wanted to feast between her legs.

But she did not kiss me back.

She did not move under me.

Still as a frightened deer, she lay prone.

The females on the compound had never lain prone.

They did what they were supposed to. They writhed, they cried, they whimpered—they submitted.

This female did none of that.

Not even in her stillness was there submission.

Yanking her head back by her hair, our mouths ripped apart and I glared at her. "What is wrong with you?"

She blinked.

No writhing, no reaction, no submission, she simply blinked. She did not even cry. All females cried when you took them the first time, but she did none of it.

"Where are the tears?" I demanded, but as I said the words, a feeling of sickness descended.

She blinked again.

"*Speak*," I barked.

Hoarse and haunting, she obeyed me for the first time and spoke. "I've never been kissed."

# Chapter
## TEN

*Shaila*

H E ROLLED TO HIS BACK, AND THE ARM THAT HAD THE shoulder I'd reset draped over his face.

Low and growly, his voice came out quieter this time. "Leave."

My lips tingling, I stared at the huge, long bulge under the boxers I'd stolen from the gas station convenience store, and I felt wetness soaking my panties. I'd diverted my eyes like a proper lady when I'd taken off his wet jeans and put dry boxers on him the other day, but I wasn't diverting my gaze now. An ache, almost impossible to ignore, was pounding between my legs and anger surged.

"You can't leave me feelin' like this," I snapped.

"Like what?" he asked, his voice an entire octave lower than a moment ago.

"Like I'm on fire," I accused.

His arm lifted and his head turned. Stark blue eyes focused on me. "You do not get to enjoy it. You endure it."

*What?* Oh hell no. My hard nipples and pulsing female

parts said otherwise. "Like hell I don't." I'd read those girlie magazines at the gas station. I was supposed to feel good, *real good.*

His eyes narrowed. "You do not cuss. You do not take pleasure unless I give it, and you do *not* disobey."

*What the ever-loving hell?* "I'm not your servant."

"You are female," he spat.

"I am a woman," I practically hollered back, equally angry and flustered by his almost naked and huge, muscular body.

"No," he enunciated. "You are not." His nostrils flared. "But take your pants off and I will make you one."

If I'd been standing, I would've stumbled back.

Make me a woman.

*Make me a woman.*

Sweet Jesus help me, I wanted to shove my jeans down right then and there. Down all the way to my ankles, because all I wanted to do was spread my legs wide and make this horrible, relentless, pounding, pulsating need in my very core go away.

But more, the possibilities opened like a cabbage rose and my mind was a flurry of thoughts. Daddy wouldn't have a virgin to sell. I wouldn't be desirable to some sick biker with a virgin complex, and the sudden fire this strange and maddening but beautiful man had lit in my body would go away.

And maybe, just maybe, if I played my cards right, he'd take me away from here and I'd never have to look back.

But those were crazy thoughts. Those were the kinds of thoughts my mama would have. Needing a man to rescue you, take care of you… be with you.

But who was really taking care of who here?

When I didn't respond, he tipped his chin once. "I smell your desire." Then he did the one thing that would send me over the edge of indecision faster than a blink of an eye.

He taunted me.

"Take your pants off."

My eyes narrowed. "You think I won't?" If you told me to go right, I went left. Always had, always would.

"I know you will not." His stare stark, his face impenetrable, he laid down the gauntlet like a professional.

And I picked it up.

Possessed by the devil, total loss of all dignity, sanity gone just like my mother—I didn't know what my excuse was, other than he said I wouldn't do it.

So I stood.

I stood so fast, all the blood rushed to my head.

Then, before sanity could take hold, I shoved my jeans to my ankles. Sitting back down, my bare naked behind hit the cold concrete floor, and I kicked my cowboy boots off. My mouth, not one to be left out by my crazy, followed suit and I made the second-biggest mistake of my life.

"Make me a woman," I demanded.

Beaten within an inch of his life, blood soaking through the bandage on his side, he didn't hesitate.

He came at me.

Quick and sure, his strong, huge hands grasped my knees and shoved them wide.

I yelped, and his mouth was on my pussy.

"Oh, sweet Jesus." I fell to the ground, and my eyes rolled back in my head.

He tongued me.

*"Oh, sweet Jesus."* I grasped at his hair with both of my hands and forgave my mother for every single second of her addiction.

Never in my life could I have imagined such a feeling.

Soaring, nirvana, tingling—one single touch from him and sanity left me.

Nothing I ever thought I would feel from a man's touch happened. I didn't hate it. I wasn't shy. I didn't feel shame. I wasn't afraid. My entire reason for breathing became this man's hands and mouth on me. His tongue, rough and firm, circled over my most private, intimate place like he'd circled through my mouth, and I started to shake.

His calloused hands moved down my thighs and I shivered.

His fingers joined his mouth, and that was all I could take.

My back bowed, my legs came off the ground, and I was a shooting star. Careening through the night toward an explosion that would obliterate me, I came.

My very first orgasm, *I came.*

My life, my hopes, my dreams—everything changed.

But he wasn't finished.

# Chapter
## ELEVEN

*Tarquin*

ONE TASTE AND SHE CONSUMED ME. Her sweet scent filled my head and my mouth, and a relentless need for more took over. She instantly became an addiction to pleasure I had been preached to and warned about my entire life.

I did not care.

Shoving her knees wide, I ate at her.

I wanted her desire coating my face, my hands, my member.

Not my member, my cock.

I was no longer River Ranch, and I did not want to *tend* to her, I wanted to fuck her.

I wanted to hold her down and fuck her until she dripped down my shaft and my seed filled her womb.

I wanted to fuck her so hard she released too many times to count.

I wanted to fuck her until she cried for me to stop.

My tongue thrashing her, my thoughts consuming my

head, I missed the telltale pulsing, and she was releasing. Constricting, shaking, her back arched off the ground and she let out a low, guttural moan.

I shoved two fingers into her and bit the center of her pleasure.

Except my fingers did not sink inside her.

They hit resistance.

Her groan turned into a scream, and she jerked away from me as she spit out an accusation. "What are you doin'?"

Conditioned by compound life, I reached to pull her back out of habit, but when I saw tears well in her eyes, my hand froze on the soft flesh of her thigh. "I am making you a woman."

A tear slid down her cheek. "That hurt."

"You are a virgin." It was supposed to hurt.

Naked from the waist down, another tear slid down her other cheek. "What do you know about it?" she asked defensively.

I had taken females and made them into women. I had taken sisters old enough to be my birth mother. For years, I participated in the nightly offerings in the men's quarters where the designated females lined up on all fours with their shifts pulled over their heads.

I knew mating.

I had been schooled on how to take a woman for as long as I could remember, because the brothers on the compound talked. Out of the presence of females and the leader, there was no subject off-limits. I knew every forbidden curse word for every act and body part, but sex was always the main topic. In detail. Most of the brothers liked to make a female cry. They bragged about their nightly takings, equating their virility to the amount of tears a woman shed. But a few of the brothers did no such thing to the females.

They coerced, they fondled, they kissed.

They made the females moan and writhe under them.

They got the women to willingly put their mouths on them.

Those were the brothers I had studied.

Those were the brothers I had learned from.

Any man could make a female bleed, but I gave pleasure while doing it. I knew how to fuck, and I had no shame. But witnessing her distress, I did not want to talk about what I knew. I did not want to think about this female in front of me, bare from the shoulders down, in the men's quarters on the compound on all fours like the designated females made to service the men nightly.

This female in front of me had never been taken, and until this very moment, that had never mattered to me.

Tears had never mattered.

But this female was crying, and it was mattering.

"Come here," I demanded, low and controlled as an anger I did not understand battled for redemption.

Her legs closed, and she shook her head. Then her gaze darted to the wound on my side. "You're bleeding again."

I did not care. "Come here," I repeated.

Indecision on her face, she bit her bottom lip. "It hurt."

I would not lie. "Pleasure is not without pain."

Her fear compounded in her expression as her eyes went wide. "Always?"

Still on my knees, one hand braced on the ground holding my weight, I did not move. "No."

"Is it going to hurt again?"

I was going to make her bleed. I was going to make her cry. I was going to hurt her again. As full of rage as I was, I relished none of it. Pushing down the undergarment she had put on me while I had been unconscious, I stroked myself. "Come here and spread your legs under me."

Her gaze dropped to my erection, and she sucked in a breath as her hand went between her legs, but she moved a fraction closer. "What are you going to do?"

Fuck her. Taste her. Break her. "Closer." Make her come again.

Her chest rose and fell rapidly, but she did what I commanded.

She sealed her fate and came a breath closer.

"Under me," I ordered, my strength waning as my blood rushed south.

Her gaze cut to my right side. "Where you were knifed, it's bleedin' again." She looked back at me. "There was a lot of mud in the wound. I tried to clean it before I stitched it." Her voice went quieter. "That has to hurt. And your ribs and your leg."

My ribs were not broken. I had experienced that before. This was not that. I was bruised and bleeding from the beating I'd taken from my brothers at River Stephens's command, and I was weak from lack of food and water for seven sunsets before I was left in the swamp for dead.

But I was neither a coward, nor feeble.

I was a man, and she wanted to become a woman.

Doing something I had never done, I used her name. "Come to me, Shaila."

Her pale skin flushed from her checks to the open

collar at her neck, and she scooted forward. Threading her legs under my chest, she rested them on either side of my thighs.

Holding her gaze, I cupped her.

She sucked in a breath, but she did not move back.

Dropping my thumb, I circled where I knew it would feel good. "You are going to release again."

Her lips parted and her eyes closed, but she did not say anything. With her legs spread and her hands on the ground behind her, she was the first female who gave me the desire to swell her body with my seed.

Leaning closer to her, I kept a slow rhythm with my thumb to give her enough pressure to relax, but not enough to stimulate her to climax. Stroking myself, I brought my mouth to her ear. "You are going to feel my hands on you." Still circling her clit, I rubbed my fingers through her soft reddish-blonde curls. "And you are going to feel me inside you." I brought the head of my cock to her entrance.

She jumped, and her voice turned to panic. "Wait."

No female had ever told me to wait. "Does this hurt?" Holding her thigh, I rubbed the head of my cock against her wet desire.

She struggled to keep her eyes open and her gaze focused as she shook her head. "No, *oh Lord*, it doesn't—"

"I am not hurting you right now." But I would. Her tightness was barely letting the head of my cock in. Breaking her natural barrier would make her bleed.

Her green eyes focused, and she looked at me like no other female had ever dared to look at me. "Right now?"

I was not just a brother on the compound. I was the digger. I was the one who buried all the secrets. I was the one who made people disappear.

I was avoided.

Except in the men's quarters after nightly prayer.

Then I was the brother who garnered a reputation with the females.

I made them wet before I even touched them.

I was told I smelled like earth and sex.

I knew where to let my breath land on their skin. I knew how make nipples hard with just a look. I knew my tongue across my own lips made them desire my mouth on them, except I had never kissed any of them.

Not on the mouth.

But I wanted to kiss this female with new-leaf-green eyes who spoke like a cursed man but trembled like a fawn.

I wanted to face her while I entered her.

I wanted to kiss her while I fucked her.

I wanted to take her smile and break it so no other man ever witnessed it.

Circling her clit, I rubbed the head of my cock through her desire again. "No pain right now."

"Oh, sweet Jesus," she moaned softly as her eyes fluttered shut. Then in the next instant, they were back open and focused on me as she gripped my arm. "You're gonna hurt me. I know you will."

I could have thrust into her.

A week ago, I would have.

But I was not in the swamp because of her.

"Lift your shirt," I demanded.

She did not lift it, but her slim fingers started to unbutton it. "You're not gonna answer me?"

"You did not ask a question." She had made a statement. I increased the pressure of my thumb because I did not want to talk. Females never spoke to me while I took them.

"It was supposed to be a question." She undid the last button and her shirt fell away from her body. "And I don't just mean physically hurt me."

Her breasts were pushed together in an undergarment the likes of which I had never seen. "Take it off." I hated it at the same time I wanted to stare at her in it forever.

She shrugged her shirt off. "You're nothing like any boy I ever met."

"I am not a boy," I growled, offended.

"Says the guy who told me he was only fifteen years old."

"I have taken many turns, maybe eighteen, maybe twenty." Maybe more. I did not start counting until I was given my first shovel as a small child and told to dig until my hands bled and my arms were too heavy to lift.

Her fingers curled around the hand I had on her womanhood and she pushed me away. "So why lie in the first place and say fifteen?"

"I do not lie."

Instead of anger, hurt spread across her face. "But you did."

My initial instinct was to not reply, to keep the compound life a secret. But I was not River Ranch anymore, and I had never conversed this much with a female. Not seeing a benefit to withholding the information, I pushed up with my good arm and leaned back on my legs. "Age is not counted since birth on the compound, not unless someone counted it for you, which was rare. When I was old enough, I began to count my own turns, but my first years were not marked. I do not know how many turns I had taken when I started to keep track, so I do not know how many in total I have aged. I knew it was at least fifteen. I did not lie."

She bit her lip and nodded. "So you gave a girl a flower?"

Cautious of her change in subject matter, I studied her a moment. "Yes."

"Why?"

I flexed the muscles on my arms. I did not know what she had done to my shoulder. It was sore, but it was no longer useless. "The female looked sad," I admitted.

She pulled her shirt in front of her. "So you risked getting the crap kicked out of you to give her a flower?"

I wanted to move her shirt away. "I did not realize there were others watching." But I should have. On compound, there was always an audience, and loyalty was reserved for River Stephens.

"Did you like her?"

She asked the question as if it upset her. I gave her the truth. "No more or no less than any other female."

"So she wasn't your girlfriend?"

I had heard the term before. I gave her the simplest answer. "No."

Her gaze drifted as she pulled her shirt closer, then she changed the subject again. "I saw the news about a raid at River Ranch a couple years ago. Were you there when it happened?"

I nodded.

"Were you...." She bit her lip. "Were you involved?"

"Every male was trained on how to use a weapon. We all took up arms when the compound was under attack." I used to think it my duty to protect the brothers and sisters.

She frowned and her gaze momentarily drifted down my body before she caught herself and looked back at me. "You didn't worry about getting shot?"

I was a man. "No."

"At all?" she asked, surprised.

"No."

Her gaze dropped to the ground, and she made a derisive sound. "Well, if I'd been your mama, I would've worried plenty for you during that raid."

No one had ever worried about me. "The sister who birthed me was deceased." I had buried her when I was nine turns.

Incredulous, she looked up. "Sister?"

"Mother," I corrected, using her terminology. I knew the language on the compound was distinct from the world outside its gated perimeter. There were dozens of members not born on the compound, and all of the elders had come to River Ranch from previous lives of sin and corruption. They often spoke about the impurities of the outside world, language being one of them.

"Your real mama is dead?"

I nodded once, not explaining the distinction in her term versus mine. I was raised to hold no more sentiment toward a female who gave me life versus the sisters who had raised me. Formative years were not held against a male once he was of mating age. Then all females became one and the same. Or they were supposed to, unless you showed a preference for one particular female, then you would have to fight for rights to her by enduring a beating. If you survived, you earned rights to the female for this life and the next, and no other brother could take her.

But that was not my life anymore, and I did not have to fight for rights to this female in front of me.

Tired, weary of conversing, telling myself I owed her nothing, I dismissed her. "I am done talking." I needed to fuck or make her leave so I could sleep.

"Oh, sorry." Putting her arms through her shirt and holding it together, she scooted back and made to get up, but paused. "Do you miss it? The... compound?"

Without welcome, a memory surfaced. River Stephens, the man who called himself my father, the brother who presided over all of River Ranch, the man I had had fearful respect for until I was nine turns around the sun, flooded into my head unwanted. I was asleep in my bunk when he had woken me in the middle of the night and told me to get my shovel.

Doing as he said, I followed him outside to find my birth mother, lifeless and beaten, lying in the dirt. Unable to cover my shock, I had daringly asked what had happened. The next words out of the Holy One's mouth were the ones that made me grow up.

*"The same thing that will happen to you if you do not do your job, digger."*

In that moment, I had vowed to never be like him, or any of the elders.

It was that same sentiment that had compelled me over seven sunsets ago to give a young, forlorn-looking female a wildflower.

But it was later that night, all those years ago, after having dragged my birth mother's body through the woods and past the usual burial grounds to where I had dug her a separate grave, that I lost faith.

I told the female in front of me the truth. "I will never miss River Ranch."

# Chapter
## TWELVE

*Shaila*

I HAD SO MANY QUESTIONS, I DIDN'T KNOW WHERE TO PUT THEM ALL. But more, I was inches away from his nakedness, a nakedness he seemed to be comfortable in, that was making both my mouth water to touch and kiss him, but also terrifying me beyond a single lick of sanity.

If only a fraction of what was racing through my blood and fluttering up my belly something fierce was what my mama felt about my daddy, then I was screwed seven ways from Sunday. With a cherry on top.

Caught up in my thoughts, his voice took me off guard.

"I am told, outside the compound, that females of birthing age make their own decisions."

I didn't even know which part of that twisted-up sentence to address. "It's a free country."

"Then decide," he commanded.

"About?" I hedged, trying my hardest not to let my gaze stray from his eyes to his bruised but sinfully gorgeous body and his larger-than-life… *everything.*

"Becoming a woman."

Oh, sweet Jesus, I had no comeback for his brand of honesty. "Maybe we should douse that fire."

Reaching forward like he had a right to touch me whenever he so well pleased, he pushed his hand between my legs and his fingers found that magic spot. "No one has ever tended to you."

Lord help me, I didn't shove him away. I didn't want to. And he didn't say what he'd said like a question, but I gave an answer anyway. "I'm not a garden."

His fingers slowly stroking my most private parts, he stared at me for a full thirty seconds. "You wanted to become a woman tonight. With me. Why?"

Embarrassed, a half laugh came out, then my mouth ran with it, sinking me further. "I can't be the first girl to ever come on to you. I mean, look at you." My hand waved through the air in the general direction of his body. "Even beat all to heck, you're...." My mouth went suddenly dry, and I cleared my throat. "You've got a lot of muscles." A whole, *whole* lot.

He didn't say a word, but his fingers continued to slowly caress me.

"Right," I scoffed, somehow managing to sound indignant while he was touching me like he was. "Of course you got nothin' to say to that." Using every ounce of willpower I had, I pressed my legs together and made to scoot back.

His hand shot out, and he gripped my thigh with shocking strength.

Then he yanked.

My ass slid across cold concrete, and in the next instant,

his hard length was at my entrance and his lips were at the edge of my ear. Desire exploded inside me like a weakness as his breath landed on my neck.

"I am going to take you," his rough voice rasped.

"Tarquin," I whispered, shivering as goose bumps raced across my flesh.

"I am going to tend to you. I am going to make you a woman." Each dominant statement he murmured in my ear was another breath-stealing swirl of his hardness through my aching need.

Panting and mindless, except for one single thought, I said the only thing I could say. "Okay."

His mouth landed on mine, his fingers pinched my clit, and he shoved into me.

Sharp, horrible pain stole my breath.

My mouth shot open, my back bowed, but no words came out. My hands flew to his biceps, and my fingers dug into his flesh as tears sprung and fell.

Oh my God.

*Oh my God.*

Hard and merciless, his thumb stroked my clit. "Take a breath, woman," he demanded, caressing the last word.

Air filled my lungs and a whimper, half terror, half plea, spilled out of my mouth. I squeezed my eyes shut. "Stop, stop, *stop.*"

His huge hand grasped my hip, holding me to him as his other hand took my face. "Look at me."

My body no longer my own, my eyes opened.

His stark blue gaze void of emotion, he stared down at me. "It is done."

Tears dripped down my cheeks, and I was suddenly that ten-year-old girl begging her daddy not to let her drug-addicted mama who'd overdosed die. "Please," I pleaded. "Stop."

His stare unwavering, he studied my tears, my eyes, my face, then his hand on my hip moved between our bodies. "Feel this."

His thumb stroked my clit again, but this time it was gentle and caressing. Then he pulsed deep inside me.

The burning pain didn't recede, but something else started to happen.

He stroked and pulsed again.

Fluttering, aching, my inner muscles moved in response to something other than pain.

His eyes closed on an inhale, and his head dipped as his mouth landed on my neck.

He tasted my tears and pulsed harder.

*Oh sweet mercy.*

A thousand feathers of the need I'd felt earlier brushed across the burning ache of my core, and my breath hitched through my starved lungs. The full scent of him filled my head. Fresh dirt, the air after a summer rain—he smelled like raw earth and musk and sin and heaven.

My taut muscles gave in to his touch.

As if knowing my legs were no longer locked, his hand moved from my face to behind my knee. He pushed my leg up and sucked just below my ear. A second finger joined his thumb, and he pulled back only to push in deeply.

"*Oh,*" I gasped, as an entirely new sensation filled my womb with a different kind of heat. A pleasurable heat.

"Feel me inside you," he growled against my neck before pulling out further and looking down at me.

My fingers still digging into his biceps, I lifted my other leg and my voice came out in a scratchy whisper. "I feel you." But I wanted something, I needed something…. "More," I begged.

His eyes on mine, he thrust deep inside me.

This time the breath he stole from me wasn't from pain. "Oh, sweet Jesus," I moaned as the burning pain became burning need.

Slow and measured, his body moved in and out of me.

His thumb and finger rolled my clit. His mouth and tongue kissed away my tears. And he did exactly as he said.

He made me a woman.

# Chapter
## THIRTEEN

*Tarquin*

**M**Y BODY INSIDE HERS, I THRUST UNTIL SHE COULD FEEL ME deep. Then I eased back and did it again. Controlling the urge to take her hard and fast, I moved in and out of her and kept my fingers on the center of her pleasure.

Her body went from rigid resistance to pure submission.

I grew harder.

I had never taken a female like her.

Her body was softer, rounder around the hips and thighs, but her womanhood was tighter, much tighter than anything I had ever felt. Her fertile body under me, her fingers digging into my flesh, her eyes locked on to mine, I had never experienced anything more consuming. I wanted to release inside her over and over.

But she needed to release first.

"Come," I commanded, dragging my nail across her sensitive flesh. "Give me your release."

Her body at my command, her core constricted, and her eyes fluttered shut. "Oh God."

"All of your release," I barked, pressing harder with my thumb.

Her legs jerked, and she spasmed around me as she cried out. *"Tarquin!"*

Hearing my name for the first time cross a female's lips as I was tending to her made every muscle in my body tense.

Then I was pounding into her as her tight contractions around my cock drove me over the edge. Pulsing harder than I ever had before, I let go and released inside her.

My chest heaving, my breath short, I filled her womb with my seed.

Then my thrusts slowed, and I did something I had never done with any female on the compound.

I did not immediately pull out.

Looking down at the woman under me, a tightness spread through my chest. Her breasts full and her nipples erect through the material of her undergarment, her cheeks flushed, her hair spilled out around her—I had never laid eyes on a more beautiful woman.

"Tarquin," she whispered, searching my eyes, her expression uncertain.

Feeling no pain, I leaned down and covered her mouth with mine.

This time she did not hesitate to let me in, and I did not take her mouth like I would take her between her legs.

I kissed her slowly.

My eyes closed, my hand buried in her hair, I suddenly understood the brothers on the compound that I had learned from. Their fixation with taking a woman's mouth, and angling them into their slow, controlled dominance was no longer an incongruity I did not understand.

Because that was exactly what I wanted.

Holding her hair, her head, I dominated her not with urgency, but with need. Need to taste her. Need to smell her. Need to feel her. Under me, around me, in the depth of my chest where my life force beat for something other than anger, I kissed her.

Her arms wrapped around my neck, and I knew.

If she were River Ranch, I would have fought to the death for rights to her.

Still inside her, I grew hard again.

A small moan escaped her mouth and bled into mine.

It was all the incentive I needed. I began to thrust into her again.

"Oh, sweet Jesus." Her head fell back as her hands fluttered across my shoulders. "What are you doing?"

I tasted the heat on her neck. "Taking you again." Grasping the back of her knee, I pushed her leg up and sank deeper inside her.

"Oh." She shuddered. "That's... *ohhh.*"

"There are many ways I am going to take you." I thrust deep and hard, wondering if I was telling the truth.

She caught my words and turned them around. "We're gonna do this again?"

"We already are." I reached between our bodies and caressed her sensitive flesh that was coated in the seed of my previous release. "You are going to give me your pleasure again."

Without warning, a tremor shook her body and she was coming.

Growling in satisfaction and need, I grasped her hip and started pounding in to her.

Her body shook, sweat beaded across mine, the sound of flesh slapping against flesh filled the old building, and I released inside her again.

My heart pounded, my breath came fast, and I held myself over her as the last pulse of my strength filled her.

Looking down at her heaving chest and flushed flesh, I stilled. "Now you are a woman."

Pink colored her already heated cheeks as her legs went limp on either side of me. "I guess I am."

There was no guessing about it. Slow, I started to pull out of her.

She gasped and her muscles tensed. "Wait," she said in a panic.

I grasped one of her ankles.

Alarm spread across her pretty face. "What are you doing?"

"Trust me." I lifted her leg and moved it across my body, gently turning her to her side. "It will hurt less this way." When her legs were together, I bent her knees up as I slowly pulled out of her.

Her mouth formed an O and she sucked in a sharp breath.

My seed and her blood spilled on to the cement floor.

She covered her face with her hands as she pulled her knees up higher. "Oh God, *that* I feel," she said, embarrassed.

"Do not be ashamed," I commanded. "It is natural." I laid her legs down and reached past her to the bag she had pulled water and food out of before. Lifting the top flap, I took one of several bottles of water and opened it.

At the sound, she lifted her hands from her face and looked at me. Womanhood flushing her cheeks, she said nothing.

My eyes on hers, I took the same ankle I had before and moved her leg back so that she was straddling my thighs again. Laying my hand on her slightly rounded stomach, I stroked my thumb over her flesh and gave a quiet command. "Spread your legs for me."

Biting her bottom lip, she let her knees fall open.

Dropping my gaze, I poured water over her swollen flesh. She jumped. "That's cold."

Resting my forearm on her thigh to hold her still, I swept my fingers through her newly tended womanhood. My gaze focused on the flesh I wanted to take again with my mouth and my body, I poured more water, cleaning her with my own hand.

A soft sound came from her throat.

I thought of taking her under running water as I cleaned her a third time.

"Tarquin," she whispered.

Still focused on where I had taken her, I drew my fingers though her soft flesh and gave her words I had never given a female. "You are beautiful." But I could not keep her.

Her small hand landed on my wrist.

Ignoring her gesture, I used the last of the water to wash her blood off me. Then, without words, without eye contact, I moved over her, put my arm under the small of her back and lifted her to my chest.

She made a shocked sound but wrapped her arms around my neck.

I crawled us to the mattress and laid her down. Turning her to her side, I brought my chest to her back, pulled the blanket over us, and slipped my good arm under her head. My body settled into the air-filled plastic and deep exhaustion hit me a second before the familiar pain in my leg, arm, ribs and side returned.

"You need to take another antibiotic," she whispered.

I had never taken medicine in my life before yesterday. Medicine was not allowed on the compound, and we were all taught to mistrust it. But I could not deny my body felt stronger after taking it than it did before. "Where is it?"

"Hand me my bag?"

I reached behind me and picked up her bag before placing it in front of her. She pulled out the packet that held the antibiotic and pushed one through the casing. Then she retrieved another medicine from a small bottle.

She handed both medicines to me, along with another bottle of water. "Here you go, antibiotic and Advil."

"Advil?"

She nodded. "It helps with the pain. And swellin'."

I took the medicines without further comment and drank the water, but saved half and offered it to her.

Watching me, she took the bottle, drank, then turned and lay back down without comment.

Following suit, I lay behind her and pulled her close with an arm around her waist. Then I gave her a single truth. "I have never slept beside a woman."

"Ever?" she asked, surprise in her voice.

"No."

"But you've definitely…." Her hand waved in front of her stomach. "You've done that before."

"Yes." I did not lie.

"A lot?" she asked, her voice catching.

I was not ignorant. I knew how male and female mating worked outside of the compound. One woman, one man, marriage was common, and females had fewer children. River Ranch was different, but I had no intention of explaining it to her.

I gave her the simplest of answers. "Enough."

She was quiet, but her breathing did not even out.

"With lots of different women?" she asked a few moments later.

I did not answer. I inhaled the sweet scent of her and touched my lips to her shoulder.

She let out a small, humorless laugh. "I'll take that as a yes."

I did not respond.

Sadness crept into her voice. "Do you want that? Lots of women? I… I heard rumors about River Ranch."

I had not thought of it until she asked, but I did not have to think twice about what I wanted. "I do not, ever again, want anything to do with the goings on of River Ranch or any of its members."

She rolled in my arms and a smile spread across her face as her hand covered my heart.

I spoke before she read into my meaning. "I cannot keep you."

Her smile dropped and her hand left my chest. She gave me

her back again. "Who said anything about for keeps? Besides, I'm leavin' here for good soon anyway. I don't have time for flowers and chocolates."

I digested her words.

I was not a conversationalist. I had not spent my days interacting with females. In fact, I did not converse much with anyone, not even the elders. I did my job in solitude, I showed up for meals and Sunday worship and nightly prayers, as we all were commanded to do, and I spent my evenings in the men's quarters before falling into my bunk exhausted every night.

I had spoken to her more than I had spoken to anyone, but I was not ignorant. No amount of conversation meant I could keep her.

I had no homestead, no job and no means.

I had been raised on the notion that paper money, formal education, society and the government were the root of all sin, and judgment day was coming. Hard work was my salvation, nightly prayer my penance, and the designated women my duty as a capable breeding male.

I was never going back to that life, and I was never giving a female a flower again.

"Go to sleep," I commanded.

"Whatever." She pulled the blanket around her as she moved away from me.

Battling pain and exhaustion, I exhaled. "You said you were leaving. Where are you going?"

"Away from here," she quipped.

I did not like, nor understand, her shortness or the underlying hurt in her voice. Females on the compound did not speak to the men like this.

"Why are you angry?" She had asked me to make her a woman. I had given her what she wanted.

Breathing rapidly, her back still to me, she jerked the rest of the blanket off me and wrapped it around her. "I ain't angry," she snapped.

I looked down at my naked body.

My torso was bound in thick white tape where she had tightly wrapped my ribs. A stab wound on my lower left side was crudely stitched, with gauze and tape over it. Another stab wound on my right thigh was also stitched and taped. My left shoulder was all mottled bruising, but the arm was now functional. My right forearm had scabbed-over shallow knife-slash wounds. From my knees to my shoulders, I was bruised.

But I was alive.

Because of her.

"Thank you," I said quietly.

"For what?" she asked defensively.

"For tending to me."

She shifted, but she did not look at me. Then she spoke in a small, hurt voice. "You're welcome."

If I had been on compound and pledged rights to her and survived the beating that would prove me worthy of her, taking her virginity and making her a woman would have been deemed an honor.

I knew nothing of the word irony until that moment.

"I am honored to have taken you," I admitted.

"Yeah, well, seems like it ain't nothin' you haven't done a whole lotta times before, so whatever. I'm not puttin' any kinda stock in that honor." She pulled the pillow out from under my head to resituate it under hers.

I stared at her back, wrapped in an old blanket with her hair everywhere. "What does that mean?"

She flipped over like a hurricane. Her face dripping tears, she spat anger at me. "It *means*," she hissed, "you dumb, infuriating, big-muscled Neanderthal, that I don't like thinkin' the man I gave my virginity to has had sex with a whole lotta other women and *taken them* before he *took me* because that makes me feel shitty and jealous, and now that we did... *that*." Her hand waved between us. "I feel all sorts of turned around in the head, and funny in my belly, and I like you a whole lot more than I should. But I'm more than a little upset that you said you ain't keeping me, because no girl who gives it up for the first time wants to hear that it's not a forever kind of love, and that her man don't want her as desperately as she wants him."

I blinked.

She made a derisive sound. "Don't that just figure. You got nothin' to say for yourself." She made to turn back over.

I cupped her nape, stopping her. "I said I cannot keep you. I did not say I did not want to."

Another tear slid down her cheek. "I don't even know what that means. *What does that mean?*"

I did not like her tears. "I have no means with which to take care of you."

She threw a hand up in frustration. "So get a job."

I did not want a job. There was only one thing I wanted besides River Stephens to breathe his last breath. "I am going to be an Army Ranger."

She stilled with surprise as her eyes widened. "You're in the Army?"

"Not yet."

"But you signed up?"

I frowned. Signed up? "No."

"So how do you know you're gonna be a Ranger? You have to like, try out and qualify for that and then train for it. I don't know much about the military, and I'm not tryin' to be discouragin', because Lord knows you look like you would be a shoo-in, but I think becomin' an Army Ranger is supposed to be one of the hardest things to do in the military. They're considered some of the best of the best, right next to Navy SEALs and those special forces, or Force Recon Marines, or whatever you call them."

Not understanding half of what she said, defiant anger surged. One of the brothers on the compound had been a former Army Ranger, and he was the smartest male in River Ranch. He could shoot a deer from a thousand yards, he knew how to build anything, the females all sought his attention hoping to be claimed, and he made every woman he took in the men's quarters sing with submission. He never spoke an untrue or unnecessary word, and not once had he thrown a single punch or kick against my flesh for my sins.

I had wanted to be like him from as far back as I could remember. But when he had come to me the morning after I buried my birth mother and made me memorize an address before telling me there were a hundred ways to take a man's life with your bare hands, I knew I wanted to be an Army Ranger. I told him as much. He had only smiled and said to remember the address.

"I am going to be an Army Ranger." And I was going to watch River Stephens take his last breath. But I was not ignorant. I knew I needed training beyond what I had learned from my compound brothers.

She stared at me for a long moment, then she simply nodded. "Okay."

My muscles relaxed marginally.

She moved closer and threw half the blanket back over me. "Did you know they got housing for spouses in the Army?" She curled into me and rested her head against my chest.

I stared at her hair as it fell across my shoulder. "Spouses?"

"Wife," she clarified.

I frowned. "You want to be my wife?"

She let out a nervous laugh. "So nice of you to ask, but I don't quite know you yet." She looked up at me, and her slight smile disappeared. "You a cheater?"

"Cheater?"

"Yeah, are you faithful?"

I stared at her green eyes. I had never seen anyone, male or female, with eyes the color of hers.

She sighed. "Faithful. As in one man, one woman, for life, till death do them part, livin' happily ever after, and never havin' sex with anyone else except each other. That kind of faithful." She paused, and her expression turned to one of shock. "Wait. Do you even know what marriage is? Do people get married at River Ranch?"

"I know what marriage means," I defended.

"So there were married couples on the compound?"

"No." River Stephens taught everyone that marriage was a false testament to God and loyalty. Bonding was stronger and lasted beyond this life. "If you claimed rights to a female, then you were bonded. It is stronger than marriage."

She frowned. "So did bonding mean you only had sex with your woman? You didn't cheat on her with other women?"

"No." I shook my head. "You would never take another woman if you were bonded. Not even if your female passed."

"Were you?" She bit her lip. "Bonded?"

"No."

Her voice turned quieter. "Did you want to be?"

I had never thought about it before I had met her. "There was never any female on the compound I wanted to fight for rights to."

A soft smile touched her full lips. "Oh."

I raised an eyebrow. "Oh?"

Heat hit her cheeks. "I like that." She laid her head against my chest again. "You never fell in love before."

I stroked her soft hair, wanting to keep her. "Go to sleep."

"Okay," she whispered, placing a kiss against my chest.

I wrapped my arms around her and closed my eyes.

# Chapter
## FOURTEEN

*Shaila*

H E SLEPT FOR EIGHTEEN HOURS.
I watched over him for every one of those hours, but by sunset the next day, I must've dozed off because when I opened my eyes, he was silently staring at me.

I smiled. "Hi."

"You changed my bandages." Rough and deep, his voice swept around me like a winter chill.

Unsure of his dark tone, I nodded. "I think the antibiotics are kickin' in. Your leg looks much better."

He flexed his leg, but he made a face. "It is fine."

"You hurtin'? I have more Advil. And it's almost time for your next antibiotic."

His stern gaze cut from his leg to me. "No Advil. Did you sleep?"

A small laugh escaped. "Seeing as you caught me sleepin' on the job, I reckon so."

He frowned. "On the job?"

"Um." I bit my lip. "Watchin' over you?" It came out sounding like a question.

His frown deepened. "I am not an infant. I do not need tending to."

"No, no, of course not." I blushed hard. "I was just...." Shoot, shoot, shoot. "Fine," I admitted, "I like to watch you sleep. I wanted to make sure you were okay. And yes, I changed your bandages as gently as possible so you didn't wake up." There, I said it.

He stared at me for what felt like a full minute. Then he issued three words that were more command than statement. "I need clothes."

"Oh, sure. I, um, washed your jeans." I reached behind me and dug in the plastic bag I'd brought in earlier from the house when I'd snuck in while both he and Mama were sleeping. "I also got you a couple T-shirts. They ain't much, they're from the gas station where I work, and the selection there is about as bad as you'd think." I laughed nervously as I held one up. "But I think it'll fit."

Sitting up without wincing, he took the clothes. "I need to bathe."

Unable to decipher his mood, I bit my lip. "Well, um, my mama doesn't know you're here, and I'm not so sure it's a good idea to go waltzing into the house and announce your presence on the way to the bathroom so you can shower."

"How did you get the mud off of me before?"

I cringed sheepishly, remembering how I'd hosed him off like a dog. "I used the hose."

He lifted his chin once and stood. "That will do." Testing his weight on his leg, he nodded to himself.

The soreness between my legs pulsed once, and I tried not to stare at all of his glorious nakedness. "It's cold water," I warned him. "Really cold."

"It will be fine." His gaze met mine. "Do you have soap?"

I tried not to stare at the man who'd taken my virginity, but he was beautiful. His blond hair was messy in a way that was masculine and sexy. His washboard abs looked like he worked out for a living, and his height only emphasized his dominant presence that was leaps and bounds beyond his age.

"Soap?" he asked again when I did not reply.

I blushed hard and awkwardly stood, still feeling the remnants of yesterday. "Mm-hm." I walked to the old tool bench where I'd put the bottle of shower gel I'd used to clean his wounds after I'd hosed him down. Picking it up, I turned to hand it to him, and he was right there.

"*Oh.*" I craned my neck to look up at him.

He grasped my chin and studied my eyes. "Do you hurt?"

Chills raced up my spine as butterflies took flight in my stomach. "No, I, um...." Sweet Lord Jesus, he was tall. And his hands were so big and rough, but his touch was so gentle it made my head spin worse than a Ferris wheel. I cleared my throat. "I'm fine."

"Pain showed on your face when you stood."

I felt the blush spread across my face and go clear down to my chest. "I'm fine."

"Did you stop bleeding?"

A lump swelled in my throat, and I remembered every second of him washing me yesterday. No one had ever shown me the kind of concern he was showing me now and yesterday, not even my mama. "Yes," I whispered.

His finger swept across my cheek. "Are you sore?"

Oh sweet mercy, he was beautiful. "A little," I admitted.

He dragged his thumb over my bottom lip. "I want to take you again."

A whirlwind came over me.

Impulsive, desperate, needy, and everything in between, I gave up trying not to touch him and threw my arms around his neck. Standing on tiptoe, I brought my lips to his with the intent to kiss him.

But the second our mouths met, he took control.

He grasped a handful of my hair, wrapped an arm around my lower back, and lifted me up into him. He angled my head as he tilted his, and he thrust his tongue hungrily into my mouth like he'd thrust into me last night.

Desire surged between my legs and curled low in my belly. I fell against his hard body and opened my mouth like I wanted to spread my legs for him.

A low growl crawled up his chest, and he pulled me in tighter. Rough and raw, he kissed me.

And Lord help me, I kissed him back.

He smelled like earth, and he felt like life. His scent rubbed across my skin and sank into my heart in a way I knew I would never forget. He was the Everglades after a summer rain, and his touch was the promise of a new sunrise. He was every wish I never got. And lifting me up, he held me like he was never gonna put me down.

I didn't just fall for him.

I came home.

Kissing me, holding me rough and hard, he stroked through my mouth one more time, but then he pulled back. His lips wet, his stare intense, he made me shiver as he kept his eyes on me and ran his hands up my legs, pushing my short skirt all the way to my waist.

Goose bumps raced across my skin as desire pooled between my legs.

Keeping his eyes on me, he and pulled my underwear down my legs. His fingers trailed a path back up, but then he dropped to squat and leaned in.

Realizing his intent, I stepped back only to hit the workbench. "No, stop."

His gaze cut from my nakedness to my eyes, and in a nonverbal way I was quickly becoming accustomed to, he raised an eyebrow to ask me his question.

My knees weak from just looking at him, I covered myself with one hand while I held on to the bench behind me for support. "I'm, um...." *Oh, sweet Jesus*, no one made me shy like this man. "I bled yesterday," I blurted.

Still in a squat, his desire standing out from his body hard and proud, he didn't hesitate. "I know."

"But...." I trailed off. Surely he didn't want to put his mouth... *there.*

"Are you in pain?"

I shook my head.

Slow and gentle, he covered my hand and moved it to my side. His mouth landed on the most private part of my body, and he swirled his tongue.

I let out a long moan, and everything in my life disappeared except him.

I didn't care about the fight with Mama, or what Daddy had planned for me. I didn't care about some biker with a stupid name. I didn't even care that I didn't know one thing about this stranger with his mouth on me where I'd never let anyone touch, because it just felt right.

*He* felt right.

Considering where he came from, I probably should've been running as far away from him as possible. Except I couldn't help but think that maybe fate put us right where we were supposed to be and two shitty pasts were meant to come together and make a better future.

Because, oh my Lord, every time he touched me, it felt like a better future was coming.

It felt perfect.

His tongue swirled over and over, making me mad with desire until I started to see stars. But before I could give him my release, he grasped the backs of my thighs. Standing to his full height in one swift movement, he brought my legs all the way up and slid his arms under my knees, effortlessly lifting me. My ass landed on the edge of the tool bench, and his hard length pressed against my entrance.

"Tarquin," I breathed.

Not speaking, his intense stare saying more than any words, he held me tight as he pushed into me.

Pain and shock and a fullness so perfect it didn't have a word stole my breath.

He drove all the way into me until I felt him hit my very womb.

My mouth opened, my voice squeaked, and I sucked in a sharp breath as every muscle in my body clenched in defense.

It hurt. It burned. It made tears well.

But then his forehead met mine, he pulled back an inch, and my name whispered across his lips.

*"Shaila."*

I lost my heart.

I lost it so bad, I knew I was never getting it back. A tear dripped down my face and my body opened up to let him in.

Slow and measured, he nodded as if he felt the very shift of the earth under my floating feet. Then he brought his mouth to my ear and whispered, "Feel me."

It was all the warning I got.

He pulled almost all the way out, then slammed into me and ground his hips like he'd swirled his tongue.

I didn't see stars.

I saw Jesus.

And heaven wasn't up in the sky. It was here on earth, in the arms of a bruised and beaten man as he plunged into me like God himself told him to.

The sensitive flesh between my legs that Tarquin had sucked now rubbed against his body as his hard length hit a spot so deep inside me that it set off a sensation I couldn't even describe.

I was flying.

Pleasure, pain, desire, need—it swirled around me and kicked into a flurry of physical sensation and emotion. I wanted to come. I wanted more. I wanted him forever and ever.

"Oh, Tarquin, *please*," I begged, gripping the edge of the rough wood workbench and lifting myself up to him for more.

He pounded into me and ground his hips two more times, and I was screaming.

His mouth slammed over mine, and his tongue drove into me like his hard length drove into my core. My back fell to the bench from the force of his thrust and kiss, and he drove into me again.

My entire body jerked, and then I was coming.

I pulsed and pulsed, my inner muscles constricting around him as he growled into my mouth. His hard length swelled, and I felt his hot release pump inside me.

Shaking, holding on to him for dear life, I submitted to his kiss and his dominance.

When he stopped pulsing, his thrusts slowed and he pushed into me as far as he could go. Holding himself there, holding me, he slowed the kiss until he gently pulled back from my mouth, but not from me or my body.

His lips an inch from mine, his eyes searched my face. "I am inside you."

Oh God. So inside me. "Yes," I whispered, smiling a smile only for him.

His expression intensified. "I will take you as my wife."

# Chapter
## FIFTEEN

*Tarquin*

**M**Y SEED INSIDE HER, HER SMILE IMPRINTED ON MY HEART, I would not let her get sold. "I will take you as my wife."

Her smile dropped and her mouth formed an O. "Wife?"

I nodded once. She said the military gave housing for that. I would be able to give her a roof over her head.

Her already flushed cheeks turned brighter. "Why, Tarquin Scott, are you askin' me to marry you?"

"No." I frowned. "I am telling you."

She let out a small feminine laugh, and her voice pitched higher. "I thought you said you understood women have a right to make their own choices," she said sweetly.

I stilled. "You do not want to be my wife?" I would take care of her. "I will provide for you." One way or another.

Her hand landed on my chest and she pushed. "Let me up."

I grasped her knees and pushed her legs up as I thrust in, before I slowly pulled out.

She sucked in a sharp breath. "Why do you do that?"

I helped her to sit up. "Do what?"

"Push my legs up like that before you leave me."

I did not like her last two words. "It makes it more comfortable for you, and I am not leaving you."

She pressed her legs together and averted her gaze. Her voice turned small and sad. "You know what I meant."

I tipped her chin so I could see her eyes. "Why are you upset?"

She drew her lips into her mouth, then exhaled. "A girl likes to be asked."

"Asked?"

"If she wants to get married," she explained in a rush.

I tucked her soft hair behind her ear. "Will you be my wife?"

A shy smile touched her lips before she dropped her head to my chest and put her arms around me. "Oh my stars, Tarquin Scott, you are not a romantic, but I swear my heart already belongs to you." She laughed quietly and looked up at me. "Yes, I will be your wife."

For the first time in as long as I could remember, I smiled.

"Oh, sweet Jesus," she whispered. "That's a sight to behold." She smiled back at me. "Why, Mr. Scott, you have a beautiful smile."

My expression sobered. "You are beautiful."

"Thank you," she quietly replied, dipping her head again. "I think... I, um...." She gave me a small laugh and crossed her ankles. "I need to clean up."

My hands on her waist, I lifted her down from the workbench. "Where is the hose?"

She nodded toward the door as she stepped out of her skirt. "Just outside. I'll get it and bring it in here. There's a drain in the middle of the floor."

"I will get it. Stay." I walked to the door, opened it, and found the hose coiled to the left. Turning on the water, I adjusted the nozzle until the spray stopped, then I scanned the surrounding property for anyone before dragging the hose into the garage. "Does anyone live out here besides you and your mother?"

"Nope, just me and Mama." She held a bottle of soap up and pointed toward the drain. "That's where I washed you off before."

I pulled the hose over and turned the water on. "Where does your father live?"

"Um, your bandages." She glanced at my body quickly, then looked away.

"I will change them." I pulled the bandages off. Her crude stitches had held. "Your father?"

"Oh. Yeah." Her voice turned impatient. "He usually lives in Daytona with his bikers at the MC clubhouse but he has other places."

"Why do you not live there with him?" I rinsed off. The water was cold, but welcome.

She waved her hand through the air. "Long story. He moved me and Mama out here years ago."

"Why?" I nodded at the bottle of soap in her hand.

"Oh, sorry." Not making eye contact, she held it out.

I took her hand and pulled her close to me. She barely came up to my chest. Brushing my lips across her forehead, I took the soap. "Spread your legs."

Her hand landed on my chest, and she focused her eyes on it. "I can wash myself."

"I know you can." I gently let the water run down her bare legs. "But I am going to show you that I will take care of you."

"Oh," she whispered.

I dropped to a knee and put soap in my hand. "Your father?" I washed between her legs.

"Yes, um...." Her hands fell to my shoulders, and she spread her legs slightly. "He moved us out here because there was lots of drinkin' and druggin' at the clubhouse, and my mama didn't know when to quit."

Rubbing my hand between her legs and across her soft flesh, I admired the curve of her hips and the fullness to her thighs. "She was addicted?" I rinsed her off.

"Mm-hmm." She closed her eyes. "She couldn't say no to drugs."

I did not comment about her mother. I stood and handed her the hose. She took it, and I quickly soaped my body and my hair.

She held the hose up. "If you bend down a bit, I can rinse you."

I bent my knees, and she held the hose over my head like a shower. I rinsed off, then took the hose from her. "Towel?"

Her eyes on my body, she inhaled, then looked up at me. "Hmm?"

I fought a second smile. "I like what I see when I look at you as well."

"Are we really gettin' married?" she blurted. "We're strangers. What if we get to know one another and hate each other?"

Before I had told her I would take her as my wife, I

had thought of the same question. I realized that if she were on the compound and I claimed rights, I would know her even less than I did now. There were rules against interacting with the females, and contact was limited to the designated females in the men's quarters at night. There were no conversations like the ones I had been having with her.

There also would not have been mating before claiming rights.

I also was sure there were no females on the compound who would have dragged a half-dead, unfamiliar male across a swamp and tended to his wounds. She had saved me. It spoke to her character. She was also forthcoming with her feelings and opinions. It was more than a refreshing change from what I had grown up with. I preferred it. She did not make the anger and resentment I carried go away, but she made it seem less important.

And my seed was inside her.

I would not leave her unattended.

Not now.

I cupped her cheek. "You saved my life. You give me honest words. You gave me your virginity, and I am inside you now. I will be a good mate. I will tend to your needs, and my heart desires to see your body grow with my child."

Her eyes welled and a tear slid down her cheek. "Did you give other women children?"

I was quickly learning I knew next to nothing about navigating life outside River Ranch, but as I stood in front of her, I knew the truth would hurt her.

I did not know for sure if I had fathered any of the children on River Ranch. The probability was there, but there were no children who looked more like me than any other of the blond men on compound.

For the first time in my life, I purposely lied. "No."

She relaxed under my touch. "I don't know if I'm ready to be a mama."

"When the time comes, you will be." She was smart and determined. "You will make a good mother." As I said the words, a desire I had never imagined a few sunsets ago grew. I wanted her with child, and I wanted to give her and that child a life I had never had. I wanted my own family.

She blushed. "Thank you."

"You are welcome."

She inhaled. "Well, we need to get you fed, and you need your antibiotic, and then I need some sleep because I'm due at work in the mornin'."

"Work?" My expression grew tight. I did not like the idea of her working.

"Mm-hmm. At the gas station down the road." She reached for a towel and began to dry herself off. "I'm a cashier. It's not the best job, but they got a pretty good convenience store that's decently stocked that I've been gettin' supplies at for a year." She handed me the towel.

"Supplies for what?"

She stepped into a pair jeans she pulled out of her bag. "Remember I told you I was gettin' out of here?"

I remembered. And I remembered why. My jaw ticked. "Yes."

"Well, years ago, I was wanderin' in the Glades west of here, and a few miles out, I found an old abandoned little huntin' cabin." She laughed. "Okay, it's more of a shack. But the roof is solid, there's a well pump outside, and nobody's claimed it goin' on three years, so I took it over." She smiled with pride. "I've been stockin' it with supplies for the past year. We can live there."

Thinking, I stepped into my pants.

She frowned. "You're not sayin' anything."

"Which direction is it?"

She pointed behind her, to the west and south. "No one goes out there. Trust me, I've been goin' out there a few times a week for the past year, and about once a month for years before that. No one goes that deep into the Glades."

River Ranch was to the north and east. I did not know how far the hunters ventured from the compound for deer, but I did not think it would be as far as she was describing. "We can go look at it tomorrow." I was still going to become an Army Ranger, but until I fully healed, I was in no position to prove my strength or stamina. An isolated cabin had appeal over the garage, where her father could show up or her mother could walk in.

"Perfect!" She smiled wide. "Be right back, I'm gonna grab us dinner." She left the garage with a smile.

I mentally recited the Army recruiter's address that the brother on the compound had made me memorize.

# Chapter
## SIXTEEN

*Shaila*

THINKING ABOUT TARQUIN, AND HOW IT'D FELT LYING IN HIS arms last night, I smiled to myself. I wiped the chipped front counter of the convenience store down with a rag, and my cheeks heated as I relived the gentle way he'd taken me after we'd eaten the simple dinner I'd made him.

*Taken.*

I smirked. I was so head over heels, I was even talking like him now. Lost in my thoughts, I missed the distinct sound of a motorcycle pulling up until it was right in front of the store. A jerk on a Harley with modified pipes made the glass windows shake.

Throwing his kickstand down, he got off his hog, and like every other biker I'd ever seen or had the displeasure of knowing, he was all attitude, leather and swagger.

His dark hair cropped close, sunglasses, and decent muscles for a thirtysomething-year-old, he walked into the convenience store with his sights set on me.

SYBIL BARTEL

I didn't recognize his cut, but I saw the one percent stitched on it, and I headed him off at the pass. "Whatever you want, I ain't sellin'." I hated bikers like him, thinking any and all women wanted to fall at their feet.

A lethal smile touched the side of his mouth as he pushed his sunglasses up. "Is that right?"

I'd learned a long time ago, the best way to deal with bikers was the direct way. "One hundred percent."

He scanned my face then my chest. If I wasn't behind a counter, he would've kept going. "Maybe I'm not buying."

"Good for you. Come of it the honest way." I'd bet every dollar I'd ever saved that there was nothing honest about him, unlike the man I'd left in my garage this morning.

The biker laughed. "I knew Hawkins's daughter would be a spitfire."

My back stiffened, and my blood ran cold. "Excuse me?"

The smirk stayed on his weathered face. "You heard me."

"Not sure I did. Because if you were referrin' to my daddy, then you best be movin' on before he hears about you hittin' on his daughter." It was no secret around here who I was or who my daddy was. And frankly, I used it when I needed it, because nothing scared away a spineless jerk like telling them your daddy was the president of the Lone Coaster Motorcycle Club.

"Is that what I was doing?" Undeterred, the biker leaned a hip against the counter. "Hitting on you?"

I didn't like his face or his scent one bit. Decent-looking or not, he was as sinister as they came, and he smelled like every other biker I'd ever met besides Daddy—oil, leather, sweat and trouble. "Better hope you weren't."

He grinned. "Why's that, doll?"

I crossed my arms and leaned away from him. "You buyin' somethin', or you just pissin' away time, botherin' a girl too young for you?"

His eyes narrowed. "How old are you?"

"None-of-your-business old."

"You legal?"

"You care?" I challenged.

He chuckled. "Fair point." Reaching to his back pocket, he pulled out a wallet on a chain, took out a twenty, and tossed it on the counter. "I'm grabbing a water. Keep the change." His heavy boots sounding across the old linoleum floor, he walked at an unhurried pace toward the cooler.

I took the twenty and rang up a bottle of water. "This ain't a restaurant. I don't need a tip."

Making his way back toward me, the water bottle dwarfed in his huge hand as he guzzled, he kept his eyes on me. When he reached the counter, he crushed the empty bottle. "I think you need more than a tip." He expertly tossed the crumpled plastic over my shoulder into the trash bin behind me.

"Nope. I sure don't." I pushed his change toward him.

Staring at me, his expression unreadable, he made no move for his money. "I think you need a clue."

Like a fool, I bit. "Yeah? About what?"

He paused for effect. Then he winked. "I'm Rush."

My stomach bottomed out and bile crawled up my throat. Then I took all of my almost eighteen years of pretending my life wasn't shit and channeled it into this one single moment. Pasting on a fake smile, I pitched my voice to stupid-girl high. "Is that supposed to mean somethin' to me, mister?"

For two whole heartbeats, he searched my face, trying to tell if I was full of shit. Then a smile the size of his hog broke out across his face. "Fuck, woman. I'm gonna love breaking you in." He slapped the counter. "Keep the change." Striding toward the door, he pushed it open, but then he paused to look over his shoulder. "Tell Stone it's a deal. I'm in." He chuckled, low and menacingly. "I'm so fucking in." Dropping his shades back over his eyes, he walked out to his Harley.

Gripping the counter for support, my chest heaved as I sucked in the air I'd been involuntarily withholding.

I didn't know how life in the Glades with Tarquin was going to pan out, but I knew one thing for certain.

My time here was up.

"Rooney!" I yelled to the back. "Get your ass out here, break's over!" I grabbed my purse from under the counter.

Watching me as he straddled his bike, Rush kicked the engine over.

*Goddamn it.* "Rooney!"

Rooney stumbled out of the back in a pot-induced stupor. "What? I was on break."

"Yeah, well, now you ain't." I shouldered my purse and hit a button on the cash register. The drawer popped open and I grabbed the stack of twenties.

"Whoa." Rooney gaped. "I'm all for sticking it to the man, but shit, Shaila. That'll get you fired *and* arrested. I'm not covering for you for *that*."

"No need to cover for me." I shoved the money in my purse. "I quit."

"Wait, wait." Rooney held up both hands. "You can't just up and quit. You need to tell boss man."

I wasn't telling anyone shit. "Bye, Rooney. It's been real."

Without a second glance, I pushed through the back door, walked down the hall and out the exit. The sun and humidity hit me like a shockwave, and I broke into a sprint, heading straight for the swamp.

# Chapter
## SEVENTEEN

*Tarquin*

S HE BURST INTO THE GARAGE IN A FLURRY OF MOVEMENT WITH bags on her arms.

I sat up, immediately on alert. "What is wrong?"

Words flew out of her mouth. "Time's up. I'm up. Game's over. Checkmate. Whatever you wanna call it, it's time *to go.*"

I pushed to my feet, taking in the curves of her body and the mud on her shoes. "What are you talking about?" My cock stirred to life.

"Rush is what I'm talkin' about. He's here. Or he was here. At the gas station. And if he's here, then there are others, and that's not good, not good at all." She dumped the bags on the floor and dragged two backpacks out from under the workbench. "Daddy won't be far behind, and if they come here together, then that's it for me."

Her rapid-fire speech, the words she used, I could not follow it. "Explain what that means," I demanded, stepping into my boots.

"I just did! We're screwed seven ways from Sunday. With a cherry on top. Well, I'm screwed. You're just...." Her hand waved through the air. "You're just beaten and stabbed. Which they'll only see as a starter for what they'll have planned for you once they find you with me." She yanked the zipper open on one of the backpacks then looked up at me with a frown. "You sure you don't got a car? A motorcycle? Anything?"

I shook my head once and pulled one of the shirts she gave me over my head.

"Whelp." She slapped her hands on her thighs as she kneeled on her haunches by the backpacks and bags. "Then we got no choice." She looked up at me. "We're goin' in the Glades."

The sound of a motorcycle approaching filled the garage.

She got up and ran to the door, lifting a corner of the material over the small window. "Oh shit."

I closed in on her and followed her gaze.

A man on a motorcycle pulled up and parked. He looked from the house to the garage.

"*Double shit*," she hissed, dropping the material and stepping back.

"Who is that?" I palmed the knife in my front pocket.

"Rush." She ran back to the bags and dropped to her knees to frantically look through them. Her hands shaking, she pulled out a handgun. Standing up, she shoved it into the back waistband of her jeans and came back to the window. "Move," she clipped in a quiet voice. "I need to see what he's doin'."

I put my hand on her shoulder. "Take a breath."

Her eyes wild, her gaze cut to me. "Are you crazy?" she whisper hissed. "Get out of my way! I need to see what he's doin'. That's Rush. *That's* the man my daddy sold me to."

I remembered the name. "I will take care of it." I pulled the gun from her waistband, dropped the magazine, and checked for bullets. It was fully loaded. I slammed the magazine back into place. "Stay here."

For one heartbeat, she went perfectly still and stared at me. "You know how to shoot?"

I nodded.

"How well?"

"My aim is true." I gently moved her out of the way of the door. "Stay here." I reached for the handle.

"He'll kill you," she warned in a panic. "I don't know what club he's from." She waved her hand toward the door. "He ain't wearin' the patch of my daddy's MC, but he's got a cut just the same, and he's a one-percenter."

I did not know what that meant, but it did not matter. My accuracy with a handgun was good, and I would protect her. "I will handle it."

"*Oh God, oh God, oh God.*" Her hands on her forehead, she paced. "You don't understand. Or maybe you do." She stopped and looked up at me. "This isn't a game to him. There's not gonna be any pissin' in the sand. He thinks I'm his, and that's all he's gonna see. You won't be able to reason with him, and if he feels threatened, he'll either kill you on the spot or call more bikers from his club to back him up and they'll kill you. Probably after they beat you." She sucked in a breath. "And you can't take any more beatin'."

I was standing, I was armed, and I was not dead. I could take plenty. "I will handle it," I repeated.

"That's it?" She threw her arms up. "That's all you gotta say? *You'll handle it?* All calm and collected, like this is a dead rat in a trap you gotta dispose of?"

Hearing the drop of his footsteps coming toward the garage door, I lowered my voice. "I do not have time to reassure you." I nodded toward a large cabinet at the back of the garage. "Go. Hide." I turned toward the door just as it was kicked open.

My arm was up and my gun was aimed before the warped wood slammed back on its hinges.

Using my one advantage, I spoke. "Rush."

Older than me by at least ten turns, the man's face contorted with anger as he reached inside his vest. "Who the fuck are you?"

"Go for a weapon, and I will shoot your hand," I warned.

"You fucking threatening me, asshole?" His tone was incredulous, but his hand paused.

"No." I did not want to bury a body today. "I am making you a promise."

"That's a goddamn threat." His gaze cut to her. "Get the fuck over here, Shaila, before I blow this motherfucker's head off."

I gave him one final warning. "She is not moving."

"Like fuck she isn't." He palmed his gun. "*Shaila!*"

I fired.

The bullet grazed his knuckles and pierced his leather vest as my woman let out a shriek.

His hand jerked, and he looked down. Fury stole his expression at the sight of his own blood, but froze his reflexes.

My aim was already on his head. "That was a warning shot. If you want to die, keep going. If you want to live, leave."

Motorcycles sounded in the near distance as the front door to the house flew open.

"Like hell, motherfucker!" He drew his gun.

I pulled the trigger a second time.

His head exploded a split second before his body dropped to the ground.

A female rushed across the driveway and fell to her knees in front of the corpse. Wild red-tinted blonde hair everywhere, she collapsed on top of the body and let out a keening cry that was drowned out by the roar of pipes.

Shaila's face twisted in panic, she threw one of the two backpacks at me. "Grab it, grab it!"

I hefted it over my shoulder and reached for the second.

She scrambled for the two smaller bags, picking one up in each hand. "Go, go, go!"

Stepping over the hysterical female and the body, we rushed out of the garage just as a dozen motorcycles came roaring around the last bend of the dirt lane.

My woman's small hand gripped my arm, and she froze. *"Oh my fucking God."*

THANK YOU!

Thank you so much for reading HARD LIMIT, the first book
in the Alpha Antihero Series!
To continue the Alpha Antihero Series, and to find out what
happens next, grab your copy of HARD JUSTICE now!

The complete Alpha Antihero Series!
HARD LIMIT
HARD JUSTICE
HARD SIN
HARD TRUTH

Have you read the Alpha Bodyguard Series!
SCANDALOUS
MERCILESS
RECKLESS
RUTHLESS
FEARLESS
CALLOUS
RELENTLESS
SHAMELESS

Have you read the sexy Alpha Escort Series?
THRUST
ROUGH
GRIND

Have you read the Uncompromising Series?
TALON
NEIL
ANDRÉ
BENNETT
CALLAN

Turn the page for a preview of HARD JUSTICE, the next
book in the Alpha Antihero Series!

# JUSTICE

One second.

That was all I needed.

My gun in my hand, my finger on the trigger, I waited.

Yesterday I was driven solely by revenge. Yesterday my life had been measured in a single act. Yesterday I did not have the taste of her on my lips. But today I wanted more than justice. I wanted the life I had been robbed of.

Except twelve men with guns drawn were standing between me and her. I should have been dead already but they made a crucial mistake. They underestimated my resolve.

I pulled the trigger.

*HARD JUSTICE is the second book in the Alpha Antihero Series, and it's Tarquin "Candle" Scott's story.

The Alpha Antihero Series:
HARD LIMIT
HARD JUSTICE
HARD SIN
HARD TRUTH

# AUTHOR

Sybil grew up in northern California with her head in a book and her feet in the sand. She used to dream of becoming a painter but the heady scent of libraries with their shelves full of books drew her into the world of storytelling.

Sybil now resides in southern Florida, and while she doesn't get to read as much as she likes, she still buries her toes in the sand. If she's not writing or fighting to contain the banana plantation in her backyard, you can find her spending time with her family, and a mischievous miniature boxer.

But seriously?

Here are ten things you really want to know about Sybil.

She grew up a faculty brat. She can swear like a sailor. She loves men in uniform. She hates being told what to do. She can do your taxes (but don't ask). The Bird Market in Hong Kong freaked her out. Her favorite word is desperate, or dirty, or both, she can't choose. She has a thing for muscle cars. But never rely on her for driving directions, ever. And she has a new book boyfriend every week.

To find out more about Sybil Bartel or her books,
please visit her at:

Website
sybilbartel.com

Facebook page
www.facebook.com/sybilbartelauthor

Book Boyfriend Heroes
www.facebook.com/groups/1065006266850790

Twitter
twitter.com/SybilBartel

BookBub
www.bookbub.com/authors/sybil-bartel

Newsletter:
eepurl.com/bRSE2T